DOG AT THE DOOR

James spun around. "Oh, no!" he whispered.

Kimble was scratching at the newspaper in her box, tearing it up, and pawing it into a small mound. As James and Mandy watched, she started panting heavily.

"Kimble?" said Mandy in a low voice. Kimble paused and glanced up.

"She's got a sort of lost look in her eyes," said James.

Kimble went back to ripping the paper. Her paws were moving faster this time, and suddenly she gave a couple of anxious whines.

"I'm going to get Mom or Dad!" said Mandy.

Read all the Animal Ark books!

by Ben M. Baglio

- ❏ BDB 0-439-09700-2 **Bunnies in the Bathroom**
- ❏ BDB 0-439-34407-7 **Cat in a Crypt**
- ❏ BDB 0-439-34393-3 **Cats at the Campground**
- ❏ BDB 0-439-34413-1 **Colt in the Cave**
- ❏ BDB 0-439-34386-0 **Dog at the Door**
- ❏ BDB 0-439-34408-5 **Dog in the Dungeon**
- ❏ BDB 0-439-23021-7 **Dolphin in the Deep**
- ❏ BDB 0-439-34415-8 **Foal in the Fog**
- ❏ BDB 0-439-34385-2 **Foals in the Field**
- ❏ BDB 0-439-23018-7 **Guinea Pig in the Garage**
- ❏ BDB 0-439-09701-0 **Hamster in a Handbasket**
- ❏ BDB 0-439-34387-9 **Horse in the House**
- ❏ BDB 0-439-44891-3 **Hound at the Hospital**
- ❏ BDB 0-439-44897-2 **Hound on the Heath**
- ❏ BDB 0-439-09698-7 **Kitten in the Cold**
- ❏ BDB 0-590-18749-X **Kittens in the Kitchen**
- ❏ BDB 0-439-34392-5 **Mare in the Meadow**
- ❏ BDB 0-590-66231-7 **Ponies at the Point**
- ❏ BDB 0-439-34388-7 **Pony in a Package**
- ❏ BDB 0-590-18750-3 **Pony on the Porch**
- ❏ BDB 0-439-34391-7 **Pup at the Palace**
- ❏ BDB 0-590-18751-1 **Puppies in the Pantry**
- ❏ BDB 0-439-34389-5 **Puppy in a Puddle**
- ❏ BDB 0-590-18757-0 **Sheepdog in the Snow**
- ❏ BDB 0-439-34126-4 **Stallion in the Storm**
- ❏ BDB 0-439-34390-9 **Tabby in the Tub**

Available wherever you buy books, or use this order form.

Scholastic Inc., P.O. Box 7502, Jefferson City, MO 65102

Please send me the books I have checked above. I am enclosing $_____ (please add $2.00 to cover shipping and handling). Send check or money order—no cash or C.O.D.s please.

Name _____ Age _____

Address _____

City _____ State/Zip _____

Please allow four to six weeks for delivery. Offer good in the U.S. only. Sorry, mail orders are not available to residents of Canada. Prices subject to change.

📖 **SCHOLASTIC**

ANIMAL ARK®

Dog at the Door

Ben M. Baglio

Illustrations by Jenny Gregory

AN
APPLE
PAPERBACK

SCHOLASTIC INC.

New York Toronto London Auckland Sydney
Mexico City New Delhi Hong Kong Buenos Aires

30322 7746

X

ISBN 0-439-34386-0

13 12 11 10 9   6 7 8 9/0

Printed in the U.S.A.   40

Special thanks to Pat Posner.
Thanks also to C. J. Hall,
B.Vet.Med., M.R.C.V.S., for reviewing
the veterinary information contained in this book.

ANIMAL ARK

Where animals come first ®

One

It was Halloween; Mandy Hope had been to a costume party in the town hall and now, as she hurried down the lane toward Animal Ark, she was remembering all the ghosts and skeletons and other creepy things she'd seen! She'd passed the row of houses behind the Fox and Goose where reassuring lights glowed from behind closed curtains. But the moon had just gone behind a cloud.

Mandy shivered and wished she'd let her best friend, James Hunter, walk home with her. She blinked to get used to the darkness, then peered ahead. Something moved stealthily out of the ditch at one side of the road. She gasped and faltered to a standstill as it came creeping toward her.

Then she smiled and crouched down, holding a hand out in front of her. "Jet! What are you up to? You nearly frightened the life out of me!"

The little black cat meowed and came eagerly toward her. As Mandy picked her up, she heard light footsteps and found herself caught in the beam of a flashlight.

"Mandy! You look really frightening in that outfit!" said Elise Knight, laughing. Elise lived in one of the houses Mandy had just passed.

"I'm the wicked witch of Welford!" Mandy whispered in a low, deep voice. "I should have borrowed Jet," she added with a chuckle. "She'd have made a fantastic witch's cat!"

"She just came for a walk with me and Maisy," explained Elise. "She comes with us every evening now. Although sometimes she doesn't stick so close by."

"Well, she really scared me!" said Mandy. She put the little black cat down so she could pet Maisy, Elise's dalmatian. "She suddenly appeared from the ditch. All I could see was a weird black shape creeping toward me!"

"It was brave of her coming up to you in that outfit!"

said Elise. "You'd think seeing that broom would have made her run."

"It's Grandpa's," said Mandy. "I think it helped me win a prize for my costume. But the others looked great, too! I left them at the end of the road. They went to trick-or-treat around town."

"I'd better get home so I can have a few treats ready in case they knock on my door," said Elise. "I don't want anyone playing any tricks on me!"

"And I've got to hurry, too, so I can have dinner ready for Mom when she comes home," said Mandy. "She's been at a veterinary convention in York all day."

Mandy walked her fingers across Maisy's nose. Maisy was deaf and had been trained to recognize hand signals. This one was Mandy's special way of saying "good-bye" to the dalmatian.

Only the dim night-lights were on in Animal Ark's clinic, a modern extension built on to the back of the old stone house where the Hope family lived. Mandy walked along the side of the building to go in the front entrance.

As she went around the corner, she thought she heard a rustling noise in the rhododendron bush. She couldn't see anything and she didn't hear the noise again. But she still went inside as quickly as she could.

The sound of music filled the small hallway. It was coming from upstairs. Mandy was glad. That meant her dad hadn't been called out. He'd be lying on the bed resting his sore ankle and maybe reading *Veterinary News* while he listened to the radio. He'd been up all the previous night with Duke, Dan Venable's shire horse, who'd had a nasty bout of colic. In his distress, poor Duke had kicked Dr. Adam in the anklebone.

Mandy went upstairs and stopped in front of the door to tell her dad she was home, but Dr. Adam was fast asleep with his sore ankle propped up on a pillow and his magazine lying open on the bed beside him. Mandy smiled and went to get out of her costume.

Before long, she had dinner ready. The soup she'd taken from the fridge was heating in the pot on the stove and there were cheese sandwiches all ready to grill.

"Now all we need is Mom!" Mandy murmured to herself. "It's eight o'clock; she said anytime between eight and eight-thirty." Then she frowned. Had she heard a knock at the front door or not? It wouldn't be her mom — she'd have used her key.

There it was again. Not a knock exactly, more of a muffled thump.

"It must be trick-or-treaters!" said Mandy as the thumping became more persistent. "All right, I'm coming," she called. She picked up a handful of candy bars to give them and went to the door.

But when she opened the door, Mandy felt her smile fade and her eyes widen in disbelief. A distraught and panting golden retriever was pulling at its leash, trying to reach the door. The end of the leash had been looped through one of the fancy wrought-iron whirls of one of the big flowerpots and the dog couldn't get it loose.

When the dog saw Mandy, it whined and strained harder at the leash, dragging the flowerpot along with a series of thumps. *So that's what I heard*, thought Mandy, stepping quickly forward.

"It's all right, everything's going to be all right." Her voice was quiet and soothing as she bent down in front of the dog.

She let it sniff her hand before stroking its soft golden head. The dog was still whimpering, but it had stopped straining quite so hard at the leash and was gazing at Mandy with imploring eyes.

"Don't worry. I'm going to unfasten you. I can't do it from here. The leash is pulling too tight. Just hang on a minute. I'll have to move around behind you."

Mandy straightened up slowly; any sudden movement would make the dog even more scared. She placed her hands carefully around the dog's body so she could unclip the leash from its collar.

Mandy bit her lip as she realized the dog was pregnant. She often helped her parents in the clinic and sometimes went on home visits with one of them. She'd seen and handled quite a few dogs who were having puppies, so she knew the signs. And from the feel of things, this poor golden retriever was very pregnant; her sides were round like a barrel and her stomach felt low and droopy. Mandy was a little worried about trying to move her on her own.

But the dog suddenly stepped backward, releasing the tension on the leash. "Good girl! I can take off the leash now! That's right, just keep still for a second," said Mandy.

After two or three attempts, Mandy managed to move the tiny knob on the clasp of the collar and release the metal ring. "There." She breathed at last. "I did it."

The dog sat down and Mandy ran her free hand over the dog's plump side. "Come on," she persuaded. "We're going inside." The dog struggled to her feet. "That's a good girl," praised Mandy. "Come on." The dog whined heartbreakingly and pulled in the opposite direction from the door.

Mandy's heart lurched; the poor dog sounded so distressed, but she knew the sooner she got her in and tried to calm her, the better it would be.

"No! *This* way," she said in a firmer tone, giving the

collar a sharp tug. Mandy heaved a sigh of relief as the dog suddenly decided to stop struggling and allowed herself to be taken inside.

Mandy kicked the front door shut behind them and led the dog down the hall and into the kitchen. She shut the kitchen door, too. She had a feeling the dog would want to try to get away again.

Mandy walked the dog over toward the stove. "You sit here." Mandy tapped the floor in front of the warm stove. "I want to see if there's a name tag on your collar. It would be much better if I knew what to call you, wouldn't it, girl?"

To Mandy's surprise, the dog sat down. There was no name tag, but Mandy did notice a triangle of black on the dog's creamy-gold chest. "That's an unusual mark," Mandy told the dog. "It might help in finding out who you belong to. But you do need a name; I'll call you Goldie. Now, I'm going to get you some water, then I'll go and wake Dad."

As soon as Mandy let go of her collar, Goldie started to wander around the kitchen, sniffing in corners and under the table and around the chairs. Then she started whimpering and whining as she scratched at the stone floor.

Mandy couldn't bear it! She knelt down in front of the dog and took hold of her front paws. "Don't do that,

Goldie," she begged. "Everything will be all right, I'm sure it will." The dog whined and licked Mandy's hand. But then she pulled her paws free and began to scratch again.

"I'm going for Dad *now*," said Mandy. She didn't want to leave the dog alone, but she knew she had to get help.

Mandy started to get up; the dog stopped scratching at the floor, whined louder and harder, and banged her head against Mandy's stomach.

"Oh, Goldie! I only want to leave you for a minute," said Mandy, trying to hold the dog's head still. "I've got to go and get some help. Dad might be able to give you something to calm you down a bit."

The dog let her head lie in Mandy's hands. But the look in her eyes was such a lost, bewildered, hurting look, Mandy couldn't bring herself to try to get up again. "We'll just have to sit here like this till Mom comes home or Dad wakes up," she said, and she thought she saw the dog's tail wag ever so slightly.

Then Mandy heard the sharp, shrill sound of the telephone. It only rang twice and Mandy let out a long breath. Her dad might be able to sleep with the radio playing, but the telephone ringing always woke him instantly.

Sure enough, a couple of minutes later, the kitchen

door opened and Dr. Adam came in. "So it wasn't a prank call!" he said, shaking his head. "Somebody just called to ask if we'd found a dog at the door," he added. And he walked slowly to where Mandy was kneeling with the golden retriever's head in her lap.

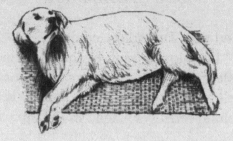

Two

As Dr. Adam came closer, the dog began to tremble and tried to wriggle herself even closer to Mandy. "She's really upset, Dad. I was going to come and get you but she got herself into such a state, I was scared to leave her."

Dr. Adam nodded. "Keep talking, Mandy. If she realizes me being here isn't worrying you, she might accept it, too."

Mandy stroked the dog's head and face with gentle fingers. "It's all right, Goldie," she said quietly. "We're going to help you." Mandy was still kneeling back on her heels and she wished she could move into a more comfortable position.

But the dog whined and kept wriggling; by now her chest and most of the front of her body was over Mandy's legs. "Keep still, girl," Mandy pleaded. "You might injure your puppies, wriggling like this. There, that's better, that's right, nice and still. You've stopped trembling! Are you going to make friends with Dad now?"

"Puppies?" whispered Dr. Adam, crouching down beside them.

"I think she's very pregnant, Dad." Mandy gulped. "She was tied up to one of the heavy flowerpots and she was dragging it along behind her, trying to reach the door."

Dr. Adam looked grim but his voice was gentle and reassuring as he spoke to the dog. "Hello, girl. There's a good dog, come on, let me have a look at you."

The dog looked at the hand he was holding out, then raised her head to look up at Mandy.

"It's okay, Goldie. Let Dad check you over." Mandy took Dr. Adam's hand in hers and drew it closer to the dog's face. "There, see, that's it . . . you're letting him pet you now . . . there's a good girl."

"I don't suppose there was an address on the name

tag?" Dr. Adam asked as he ran his hands over the dog's back and sides.

"There isn't a name tag." Mandy shook her head. "I just had to call her something. I don't know why, it didn't seem right saying 'dog' or 'girl' all the time. Not when she was feeling so alone. And, who —"

Mandy forced herself to stop talking. She wanted to ask "Who could have done a thing like this?" But she knew the anger would have shown in her voice and that would have worried the poor animal even more. Instead, she watched with anxious eyes while Dr. Adam continued to run his hands over the dog.

"Her abdomen is very saggy," he said, glancing up at Mandy. "You're right, she is *very* pregnant. In fact," he stroked his beard thoughtfully, "I think the pups are due any day now. I'll need to give her a more thorough examination. But for now . . . has she had anything to drink?"

"I got the milk out of the fridge, but that's as far as I got," Mandy told him. She sighed with relief as the dog moved off her legs.

"Don't move too far away from her," said Dr. Adam. "She's calmed down a lot and her breathing's not so panicky. I'll warm some milk and bring it over."

Dr. Adam placed the bowl of milk in front of her a few minutes later. At first, the dog just stared at it. Then Mandy saw her lick her lips and she held her breath as Goldie got to her feet. But she just sniffed at the bowl and then turned her head to gaze at Mandy with reproachful eyes.

"What's the matter, girl? Don't you like milk? Maybe she wants water, Dad. I think she wants *something*."

But the golden retriever didn't even bother to sniff at the bowl of water when it was offered.

"Come on, Goldie," Mandy said, slowly petting the dog. "At least drink a little."

Finally, the golden retriever bent her head down to the bowl.

"Well, she's not overly enthusiastic, but at least she's drinking it," said Mandy.

As they watched the dog slowly lapping, Mandy asked her dad about the phone call.

"I'm almost sure it was from a phone booth," said Dr. Adam. "I could hear traffic in the background. It was a woman, and she sounded upset, but she only asked if we'd found a dog at the door before hanging up."

"Do you think Goldie's *her* dog? Do you think she abandoned her? Or could she have *stolen* Goldie and panicked when she realized she had a pregnant dog on her hands?"

Dr. Adam didn't have time to answer. Goldie suddenly lifted her head from the bowl and stared intently toward the door.

"It's Mom!" said Mandy, moving swiftly. "I'd better warn her to come in quietly." She intercepted her mom at the door and explained the situation.

"I can't leave you two alone for a second, can I?" Emily Hope was shrugging off her outdoor coat as she spoke. She wasn't looking at her daughter or her husband; her green eyes were on the dog.

Mandy caught her father's gaze. The golden retriever hadn't moved, but she was looking at Dr. Emily and her long, feathery tail was moving ever so slightly.

"Are you coming to say hello?" Dr. Emily stayed where she was, crouched down, and held her hand out. "I want to see if she'll come to me," she said quietly. "Do we know her name?"

"I call her Goldie," Mandy replied.

"I don't think your mom's going to have to call her anything," Dr. Adam whispered.

Mandy nodded and smiled. The dog was walking slowly but surely toward Dr. Emily.

"She's a beauty," said Dr. Emily. "Well cared for, too, from the look of her. But she's worried and disorientated, aren't you, girl! You're with strangers and there are no familiar smells, or toys, or rug for you. Poor Goldie."

"I don't think Goldie really *is* her name," said Mandy.

"It will do for now." Dr. Emily was still concentrating on the dog, who was moving closer and closer.

Mandy held her breath as she watched to see what would happen. When Goldie reached Dr. Emily, she sat down. Then, with her head slightly to one side, she lifted a paw.

Mandy felt a great big lump in her throat while she watched the two of them. The dog's brown eyes held such a sad look as she sat there with her paw trustingly in Dr. Emily's hand. They stayed like that for a few seconds, then Goldie withdrew her paw and stood up. She looked over toward Mandy and Dr. Adam before walking over to them.

"An encouraging sign," murmured Dr. Adam. "Don't move yet, Mandy. Let the dog play it her way."

This time the dog gave a little grunt as she sat down and held up a paw. She was looking at Dr. Adam, so he stepped forward first.

"Still wary of me, aren't you, girl!" he murmured, noting the slight trembling and the speed at which the retriever withdrew her paw. "I don't think she's used to men," he added, glancing at his wife as he moved away.

"Mmm, she definitely seems to relate better to females." A small smile touched Dr. Emily's lips as Goldie shuffled, still sitting, a couple of inches closer to Mandy.

Mandy knelt down in front of Goldie before taking her paw. She was pleased to see that the dog's eyes were starting to lose their hurt expression. "She must be feeling safe with us now," said Mandy, using her free hand to play gently with the soft fur on Goldie's chest.

"She needs a closer examination than the one I gave her," said Dr. Adam. "And we need to check to see if she's been microchipped."

Mandy knew that a lot of owners had a numbered microchip injected painlessly into their pet's neck. Most vets, police stations, and branches of the SPCA had a special scanner they could use to reveal the number. "I hadn't got around to thinking of that!" said Mandy. "If Goldie *has* been microchipped someone will be able to trace her owner, won't they?"

Dr. Emily nodded. "Either way, we'll have to inform all the authorities as soon as we know. I think it would be best if you and I handled her, Mandy. Let's see if we can get her to come through to the clinic."

"You could finish making dinner, Dad," said Mandy. "The sandwiches are all ready to toast. Poor Mom must be starving!"

"I am," agreed Dr. Emily. "But as always it's —"

"Animals first!" laughed Mandy and Dr. Adam together.

"No microchip," reported Dr. Emily, after she'd run the scanner over Goldie's neck. "And no name on her collar, either. Put it back on, Mandy. Then you can hold her steady while I listen to her heart and lungs."

Mandy watched Dr. Emily's expression carefully and smiled when her mother gave a satisfied nod. "No problems there," she said. "Ears, eyes, mouth, and nose are fine, too. I think she's about eighteen months old. And this is probably her first pregnancy."

"Her nails feel naturally short" — Mandy leaned over to feel for herself and Dr. Emily continued — "so it seems as though she's used to walking on sidewalks or rough roads. Indoor dogs, or ones who only have a yard for exercising in, usually need their nails trimmed with clippers."

"Goldie's turned out to be a good name for her," chuckled Mandy. "She's being as good as gold. She doesn't seem to mind being up on the examination table at all."

"Not up till now." Dr. Emily smiled and reached for a pair of rubber gloves from the cart. "She might not be so happy at this next part, though. I want to take her temperature."

Mandy watched as her mother got a snub-nosed glass thermometer, then spoke soothingly to Goldie. The dog flinched a bit but she didn't struggle. "There, I'm proud of you," Mandy whispered.

"It won't take long, girl," murmured Dr. Emily.

"Is her temperature okay?" asked Mandy half a

minute or so later when her mother removed the thermometer.

"Slightly below normal, just a little over ninety-eight
point six."

"Is that something to worry about, Mom?"

"Not in the way you think. A normal temperature is
around one hundred or one hundred two. But in a pregnant dog, a dropping temperature is one of the signs
that the pups are within a day or two of being born."

"Dad thought they were due any day," said Mandy as
she helped Dr. Emily lift the heavy dog from the table to
the floor. "What are we going to do, Mom? What if nobody's reported her missing? Where will she go to have
her pups?"

Dr. Emily took a leash from the hook on the door and
clipped it onto the dog's collar before replying. "One
thing at a time, Mandy. We'll take some food in with us.
You can make her a meal while Dad and I sort a few
things out. Come on, girl," she added, patting the top of
her leg to encourage the dog to follow her.

She passed Mandy a can of special care dog food and
a packet of dry food from the display in the reception
area and the three of them walked through the connecting door back into the kitchen. But Goldie whined
anxiously and pulled toward the back door.

"Shall I take her into the yard, Mom?" Mandy asked. "I'll keep her leash on but she can't get out anyway. The gate's shut; I came in that way."

"Yes. Keep a good hold on the leash, though I don't think she'll try to run off. She might just have to go to the bathroom. Leave the door open and call out if you need any help."

Sniffing here and there, the golden retriever walked around the yard for a while before crouching down. "Good girl," praised Mandy. "Should we go back in now and get you something to eat?"

Goldie seemed only too anxious to go back inside. And when Mandy unclipped the leash, she went straight for the spot in front of the stove.

Dr. Emily was munching a raw carrot. "Just something to snack on," she said. "Your dad's gone to make a few phone calls. The kettle's boiled and I've put some yeast extract in that jug. You can make some gravy to soak the dry food in."

"How much of everything?" Mandy asked.

"Just soak a very small handful of the dry food. Then mix it with a quarter of the canned meat."

"Are we not giving her much in case the food doesn't agree with her, Mom?"

Dr. Emily smiled. "That would be a reason, normally. But even if we knew what Goldie's usual diet was, we'd still only give her a small portion to prevent her from feeling bloated. At this stage of pregnancy it's best to feed a dog little and often, rather than giving her one or two main-sized meals. And it wouldn't surprise me if Goldie didn't want anything to eat at all."

"Because she's in a strange place, Mom?"

"That could be a reason, of course. But refusing food is another sign that the pups are only a day or two away from being born." Dr. Emily smiled. "We'll see what happens when you give her some."

"Who's Dad calling?" asked Mandy as she opened the can.

"The police, the dog warden, the SPCA, Betty Hilder, and the Golden Retriever Rescue." Dr. Emily smiled. "Though, unless it was a dog thief with an attack of guilty conscience who called, which is extremely unlikely, I very much doubt there'll be any report of a missing golden retriever that matches the description of this dog."

"What comes next, then?" asked Mandy. She kept on mixing the dog food but turned her head to look down at Goldie. The dog was lying on one side, her body slightly curled and her legs stretched out. She'd crossed one front paw over the other, her head was resting on the floor, and she was watching Mandy.

Mandy stopped what she was doing and kneeled

down beside the dog. Goldie licked Mandy's hand and gave a little whine.

I just hope that nobody's coming to take her away to the dog pound, thought Mandy as she played gently with Goldie's ears.

Three

"It's all arranged," said Dr. Adam. He was limping slightly as he walked back into the kitchen.

"What is?" Mandy asked anxiously.

"Betty Hilder says she could have Goldie and her litter at the animal sanctuary. She thinks she'd probably be able to find homes for the pups when they're old enough. And the Golden Retriever Rescue would be willing to take Goldie. That's unless someone claims her, of course, which I doubt."

"We won't be taking Goldie to the animal sanctuary tonight, will we, Dad?"

Dr. Adam smiled at his daughter. "No. Unless she's

claimed, Goldie's staying here to have her pups," he said.

"That's great!" said Mandy, dashing over to give him a hug. "Does Mom know? She went to take a quick shower. What's the matter?" she added as her dad gave a small gasp.

"You knocked me off balance a bit, sweetheart, and my ankle isn't feeling so good."

"Oh, Dad! I'd forgotten all about Duke kicking you. Tell you what . . ."

Mandy took the first-aid box down, then handed Dr. Adam a tub of anesthetic cream. "Sit down and rub some of this on your ankle while I finish with dinner." She turned to glance over at the golden retriever. "I don't think Goldie wants hers."

"Don't worry about it, Mandy. Expectant moms often go off their food a couple of days before the pups are due."

Mandy nodded. "That's what Mom said. But I'm worried that she feels too strange and unhappy to eat."

"Well, we'll see how things develop. In the meantime, let's try to make sure she drinks a reasonable amount of fluid."

Dr. Adam gave a little groan as he started to rub the cream in, and immediately Goldie waddled over to him.

She sniffed at his ankle, then, whining a little as though in sympathy, she licked his hand.

"Well, I don't know whether you feel sorry for me or if you just like the smell of the cream," Dr. Adam said softly. "But you're a good, brave girl, aren't you!"

"She's thanking you for letting her stay to have her pups," said Mandy. She smiled as Goldie allowed Dr. Adam to rub the top of her golden head before turning to waddle away. "Dad, do you think her owner *did* abandon her? How could anyone bear to? She's such a loving, gentle animal!"

"She's also having puppies," Dr. Adam replied grimly. "Maybe her owner hadn't bargained for that!"

"But they'd have noticed before now!" said Mandy. "I think she was stolen and the thieves panicked when they realized she was pregnant."

"In that case, she'll be reported missing." Dr. Adam shook his head. "Only time will tell, Mandy."

Mandy nodded. "Look, she's settling down in front of the stove again. I'll get my big beanbag for her later. We can put an old blanket and a sheet over it. And what about —"

"Mandy! Dinner?" prompted Dr. Adam, smiling. "I'm sure that soup is more than ready by now, and I toasted the sandwiches while you and Mom were examining

Goldie. They're on a baking tray in the oven. If we don't eat them soon, they'll be soggy."

"It'll be a bit of a struggle getting them out," Mandy chuckled. "There isn't that much room between Goldie and the oven door."

In the end, Mandy had to kneel down and stretch over the big dog to get the tray of toasted sandwiches out. "It's all right, just you keep still," whispered Mandy.

Goldie blinked sleepily, then yawned; other than that, she didn't move a muscle.

"That soup smells good!" Dr. Emily hurried in, looking pink and warm. Mandy hid a grin. Her mom's cheeks were clashing terribly with her red hair, which was tied up on top of her head. "You look pleased, Mandy," Dr. Emily said. "I guess that means your dad got the okay for Goldie to stay a while?"

Mandy nodded and carried the soup bowls to the table.

"What I want to know," said Mandy, once they were all eating, "is why you're letting Goldie stay at Animal Ark for the next few days. You're usually so strict about not taking in strays. Not that I'm complaining, of course," she added with a happy smile.

"Special circumstances," Dr. Adam replied. "If it's the dog's first litter, and we think it is, she might need help when the pups start to arrive. Especially after what she's been through this evening. Letting her go to another strange place with another bunch of strangers, well . . ." Dr. Adam shook his head.

"Your dad and I agreed that it would have caused her too much distress," said Dr. Emily. "And moving Goldie around could send her into labor before she's completely ready."

"I think it's unlikely she'll start for a day or two," said Dr. Adam. "But first thing tomorrow, we'll have to organize things. We should fix up a good place for her to have the pups and try to get her familiar with that place before anything happens."

"What do you mean, fix up a good place?" Mandy asked.

Dr. Emily smiled. "It will be easier to keep an eye on her if she's in the house," she said. "Besides, she might settle in better if she feels like part of the family while she's here. Though I think it would be sensible to confine her to the kitchen. It's close to the yard and it's the best room to arrange a birth area in."

"I'll call James first thing in the morning," Mandy said eagerly. "He'll be really glad to come and help. That's if you don't think seeing another new face will upset Goldie."

"She'll probably be happy to meet James," said Dr. Emily. "Golden retrievers are popular family dogs because they like having people around them. And she'll be able to smell Blackie on him, which should help."

Blackie was James Hunter's black Labrador. James had had him since he was a tiny pup, so he was used to handling dogs. He loved animals almost as much as Mandy did; the two of them had often worked together helping ill or injured animals.

When they'd cleared the dinner dishes away, Mandy got the big beanbag from the corner of her bedroom, as well as a soft old blanket and a sheet. "This is your bed, girl," she told the dog. Goldie lifted her head to glance at it, then closed her eyes and went back to sleep.

"Just leave it there. She might decide to use it later," said Dr. Emily. "And listen, Mandy, I don't want you to keep coming down in the night to check on her. I'm sure she won't go into labor just yet, but I'll look in on her a couple of times anyway. All right?"

Mandy knew from her mother's firm tone that she really meant what she said.

"All right," she agreed. "But how about if I get up early? I'll take Goldie into the yard if she wants to go and I'll give her some milk afterward. I can get all my chores done early as well, then I'll call James. That would be okay, wouldn't it, Mom?"

"Fine," Dr. Emily replied, and Mandy went happily to bed.

*   *   *

The next morning, James arrived at Animal Ark ten minutes after Mandy had called him. She'd told him not to knock on the back door but to come right in. "That way, Goldie will think you're one of us," she'd said.

So James, slightly out of breath and his eyes bright behind his glasses, walked in and went straight over to sit at the kitchen table. "Dad's changing the front wheel on my bike," he said. "I ran all the way here." James lived at the other end of the town.

At the sound of his voice, the golden retriever lifted her head from her paws. She looked at him steadily for a moment, then lowered her head again.

James smiled. "Not exactly a big hello, but at least she isn't bothered that I'm here. She's very pretty, Mandy. She's got such a gentle-looking face."

"She's got a nice, gentle nature, too," said Mandy. "She really likes it there in front of the stove, James. I took her out in the yard early this morning, then persuaded her to drink some milk when we came back in. She didn't want any food, but Dad said not to worry about that. After she'd had her milk she went straight back there to lie down. She's completely ignored the beanbag bed I made for her."

"She's probably used to lying in front of a stove wherever she's come from." James looked from Goldie to Mandy, a look of disbelief on his face. "Do you think she *has* been abandoned, Mandy?"

Mandy shrugged helplessly. "Dad's called all the places he contacted last night and there's still no report of a golden retriever missing from home," she said. "But if she was stolen, it might have been miles out of our area."

James scowled and shook his head. "It doesn't take long for information to reach other counties," he pointed out. "They use computers to do that."

"Well, all we can do is to make her feel as good as possible," said Mandy. "And to fix up a special place for when she has the puppies."

"I've been thinking about that!" Dr. Adam came in just in time to hear Mandy's last words. He smiled at James, then pointed to a large cabinet a couple of yards away from the stove.

"We could pull that out. I'm sure we can find somewhere else to put it temporarily. And I bet one of those special boxes for when a dog or cat has a litter would fit perfectly in the space. The single cupboard will separate it from the stove, so that area will be nice and warm without being too hot."

"Have we got a spare one in the clinic?" Mandy asked.

"No. We need to keep ours in case of any emergencies. But luckily," Dr. Adam grinned, "the man who works for the company that makes them lives in Walton."

Walton was only two miles away from Welford; Mandy and James went to Walton Moor School there. They weren't in the same class; James was a year younger than Mandy.

"I've already called him," Dr. Adam continued. "He's agreed to bring his sample model over. All we need to do is assemble it."

"Dad! You're brilliant!" said Mandy. "Come on, James, help me drag the cabinet out!"

"Uh, Mandy." James shoved his glasses farther onto his nose. "Doesn't your mom keep dishes in that cabinet?"

"Yes, but . . . Oh, I see what you're getting at!" Mandy laughed. "You're right, James. We'll have to empty it first!"

"That's up to you two," said Dr. Adam, ruffling Mandy's hair. "I've done my part for now. I've got to make a couple of home visits. One of them's to Yindee. *Another* upset stomach!"

Mandy chuckled. Yindee was a Siamese cat with a habit of eating wool. No matter how hard her owner tried to hide wool sweaters from the Siamese, Yindee somehow managed to find every new hiding place.

She'd claw at the garment until the wool started to un-
ravel, then bite off and eat all the loose bits.

"Make sure you keep your jacket on while you're
there, Dad!" Mandy glanced meaningfully at the warm
wool sweater Dr. Adam was wearing.

"Will do," he replied cheerfully. "Hello, girl," he added
softly. Goldie had raised her head again and was looking at him. "Do you want me to pet you? Have you decided I'm not too bad after all?"

"She wasn't sure of Dad at first," Mandy told James as
they watched Dr. Adam petting the dog.

"I bet she came around soon though," said James.
"Both your parents are great with animals!"

As Mandy nodded, she noticed that Dr. Adam's hands
were moving slowly over Goldie's barrel-like sides.

"Everything *is* okay, isn't it, Dad?" she whispered
anxiously.

"As far as I can tell, everything seems fine, sweetheart. Just make sure you take her outside as soon as
she shows any sign of wanting to go."

"Okay," said Mandy. "We'll empty the cabinet and see
if she wants to go out before we start moving it." She
smiled as Goldie pawed at James's sneakers.

A look of delight appeared on her friend's face and he
bent down to pet the dog. Mandy guessed he'd been long-

ing to do that, but James was good with animals, too;
he'd known to wait until Goldie *wanted* him to pet her.

By the time Desmond Barratt, the sales representative,
arrived at the back door with the special box, Mandy
and James had finished preparing the small area it was
to go in.

"I won't come in, Mandy," Desmond said quietly. "It
might upset the poor girl, seeing another stranger. The
box is easy enough to assemble; everything slides into
place. There's an instruction sheet with it so you
shouldn't have any trouble."

Before long, the parts of the box were spread out all
over the kitchen floor. Mandy and James were on their
knees, reading over the instruction sheet, when Goldie
got up and walked toward them.

"You know, Mandy," James said thoughtfully, "that
leather collar looks awfully heavy for her to wear all the
time."

"You're right, it does!" Mandy got up. "I'll go over to
the clinic and get a lightweight one for her."

Jean Knox, Animal Ark's receptionist, glanced up
when Mandy hurried through the connecting door. She
knew all about Goldie, of course. If anyone happened to
call about the golden retriever during office hours,

she'd be the one to answer the phone. "Everything okay?" she asked. "No problems? Your mom's with a patient but I could get Simon for you." Simon was the nurse.

"No, no problems, Jean," Mandy assured her. "But Goldie's wearing a heavy collar. She could use a lightweight one. Will it be okay if I take one from the sales display?"

"I'll buy it for her, Mandy. I'd like to do something to help."

"Thanks, Jean," Mandy smiled. "I'll tell Goldie that it's a present from you. I'll have a blue one, please."

Mandy hurried back to the kitchen with the new collar and showed it to Goldie. "This will be comfier for you," she said. "You owe James and Jean a lick!"

Mandy removed the leather collar and put it on the floor beside her. Then she put the new one around the dog's neck. Goldie whined and walked slowly toward the back door.

"You take her, Mandy," said James. "I think I've figured out where everything goes, and it'll be easier putting it together with Goldie out of the way. She was getting interested in all the different pieces while you were gone. She kept sniffing them."

"That's good!" said Mandy as she opened the back

door. "Let's hope that means she'll be happy to use it when it's ready."

Goldie made her way to the end of the yard and went to the same place she'd used before. "Good girl," Mandy told her. "You're starting to make a nice little routine for yourself, aren't you! How about staying out a while longer? Give James time to put your special box together?"

But James suddenly appeared at the back door. "Mandy! Mandy!" he called urgently. "Come here — quick!"

Four

"What's up, James?" Mandy demanded, racing to the back door and turning to wait for Goldie, who was meandering slowly up the path.

"I was picking her leather collar up off the floor and I suddenly thought of looking at the underside," James said quickly.

"Mom and I looked there after we checked to see if she'd been microchipped." Mandy sighed. "I thought someone had called to —"

"Mandy!" James interrupted tersely. "There *is* a name on it!" He dangled the collar in front of Mandy's eyes. "I'd never have seen it if I hadn't been looking really closely. I think somebody scratched it on with the point of a needle or something!"

"Where? Let me see!" Mandy almost snatched the collar from him in her impatience.

"There!" James pointed triumphantly to some very faint, scratched lettering.

Mandy squinted in concentration; she had to hold the collar at several different angles before she could make the letters out. "Looks like K . . . I . . . M . . . S . . . L . . . E . . . I . . . O," she said doubtfully. "That doesn't sound like a name!"

"I don't think the last two are letters. I think they're numbers!" James told her. "There's a space after the E; maybe somebody was going to scratch the address on as well. And it isn't an S there, it's a B!

"Whoops!" he added as the golden retriever nudged his legs with her nose. "Sorry, girl, are we in your way?" James moved aside to allow her to walk through the door.

"B," said Mandy. "That would make it" — Mandy figured it out — "Kimble." she said. "Wow, James! You're a genius!" Mandy just managed to stop herself from hugging him; James got embarrassed so easily.

"There's a Jessica Kimble in the first grade at school, isn't there?" Mandy went on excitedly. "Her dad breeds birds and I'm sure they don't have a dog. But it's an unusual name. She might have a relative who does. We could call and ask. She lives in Walton."

"That's what I thought!" James nodded. "And if she doesn't, we can look for Kimbles in the phone book."

"Keep an eye on Goldie," said Mandy. "I'll go and tell Mom about your discovery and I'll get the phone books. I'll bring all of them, in case we need them. We've got one for every county in North Yorkshire!"

"Well, I'm glad it's a fairly uncommon name," James murmured to Goldie. "Hey, no, come away from there, girl. I've still got the front part and one of the side parts to put in place!"

The dog had gone to the partially assembled box and looked as if she was about to try to get into it. James knelt down and rubbed his face against the soft fur on the retriever's chest. She whined, and when James lifted his face, she licked his cheek.

"Oh, Goldie!" James had to take his glasses off and give them a good rub.

Mandy seemed to be taking her time, so with the golden retriever watching his every move, James finished assembling the box. "We should let Dr. Adam or Dr. Emily check it before you get in," he said. "I'll lift it onto the table for now."

Goldie watched him with mournful eyes, and James swallowed hard. The dog looked so sad!

"Sorry to have taken so long, James." Mandy returned, carrying four telephone books. "Mom called Jessica's dad; he's one of our clients. They don't have any Kimble relatives in this part of the county, so it's down to searching for ourselves. Mom said to start checking in the local directory," she told James. "But she doesn't want us to call anyone. She says it will be best if she does that. Office hours are finished, so she'll be here soon."

"Well, the local one only covers places within fifteen miles or so from here. If we don't find the right Kimble in that, I hope she'll call all the Kimbles in the rest of the county!" James said fiercely as he crouched down next to the dog.

Mandy gazed at him in astonishment. James was usually so calm and even tempered.

"Sorry," he muttered. "I know your mom will do that if she has to. It's just that . . ." James buried his face against Goldie's chest again. "She's such a good dog," he said in a muffled voice. "I think she likes the box. She tried to get in it!"

"It looks great, James," Mandy told him, then she flipped through the pages of the local directory until she came to the K's. "There's five entries under Kimble."

she said. "Two in Walton — but one's Jessica — two in Glisterdale, and one in Upper Barnall. So that's four to try. Oh, I hope Mom doesn't take long!"

"Impatience should be your middle name!" Dr. Emily spoke from behind her daughter and Mandy turned to grin at her.

"I didn't hear you come in," she said.

"I'm not surprised. You were too busy talking. Did you say there are four Kimbles to try?"

Mandy nodded as her mom pulled out a chair and sat down. "*If* we happen to find Goldie's owner," she said, "I'll have to report to the SPCA and let them take things over from there." She smiled and added gently, "I know you're hoping we'll be able to return Goldie because she was stolen. But if someone claims her, we'll need to be very sure that is what happened."

"You mean if she hasn't really been stolen, the owner might take her back and abandon her somewhere else?" asked James.

"I'm afraid so, James. That's why we'd have to let people who are used to handling this sort of thing deal with it." Dr. Emily got up and went over to the phone.

When Mandy read out the first number, James got up from the floor where he'd been sitting with his arm around Goldie and joined her at the kitchen table. Their eyes were glued to Dr. Emily as she spoke to someone on the phone. Even though they could only hear one side of the conversation, it was obvious that this Kimble didn't know anything about a golden retriever, missing or otherwise.

The second call was no good, either. Mandy read the third number out. This time, Dr. Emily seemed to be having trouble making herself understood.

"I'd like to speak to Mr. or Mrs. Kimble, please," she repeated. Then she gave the number she'd dialed. "Yes that number is listed next to the name Kimble. Initial . . ." She glanced at Mandy who told her. "Initial P," Dr. Emily said into the phone. "Oh, I see. Yes, well, I'm very sorry to have troubled you."

She replaced the receiver and grimaced at Mandy and James. "There's no Kimble there and there never has been," she reported. "And he doesn't know anyone called Kimble, either. I think he was telling the truth," she added wryly.

"It must be a misprint," said Mandy. "Let's try the last one."

"The last *local* one!" James corrected.

Goldie had wandered over to the table and plunked herself down in between him and Mandy. James was petting her but he kept his eyes on Dr. Emily. From the look on her face this phone call was more promising.

"You say your son's got a golden retriever?" said Dr.

Emily. "And she disappeared three weeks ago? Yes, yes, please, I would!" She reached for the pad and pen next to the phone.

Mandy clutched at James's arm. This could be it! If Goldie had been stolen three weeks ago, and the thief hadn't realized the dog was having pups until yesterday . . .

Dr. Emily turned quickly from the phone. "She's looking up her son's phone number. She can't remember it. I think she's very elderly," she added with a whisper.

Then she said, "Yes, I'm here, Mrs. Kimble!" Dr. Emily started to write.

But Mandy saw her mom's hand falter; saw her shake her head. She glanced quickly at James just as Dr. Emily said, "Mrs. Kimble? Does your son live in *Australia*?"

Emily Hope had recognized the area code immediately; the Hopes had done a six-month exchange with a veterinary practice in New South Wales and they still kept in touch with the Munroes at the Mitchell Gap clinic.

"Australia! How could anyone think that a dog lost in Australia could end up here!" Mandy groaned despairingly. She was so disappointed. James let out a huge sigh and reached for one of the other phone books.

"Cheer up, you two," said Dr. Emily. "Poor Mrs. Kimble was only trying to help! I told you she sounded elderly," she said, glancing reprovingly at her daughter.

"Sorry, Mom," said Mandy. "I suppose at any other time I'd have found it funny," she admitted. "But I was so sure we were going to find the right Kimble this time."

She turned to Goldie. "Hey, what's the matter, girl? You shouldn't jump up like that, not in your condition!"

Goldie was trying to get her front legs onto Mandy's lap. She was looking intently at Mandy and she was panting slightly; her long pink tongue lolling out at one side of her mouth.

"Maybe she's trying to get into the box," said James, glancing up. "She did try to get in it before, Dr. Emily, but I wanted you to check it first to make sure I've done everything right."

Dr. Emily smiled. "Okay, I'll do that now. But it looks fine, James."

James blushed, then turned to Mandy and said, "There's only one Kimble in this phone book! I haven't —"

"James!" gasped Mandy. "Say that again, will you! Just the first part."

James gave her a puzzled look, but he did as she'd asked. "There's only one Kimble in this phone book," he said.

Goldie jumped up again. "I *was* right!" cried Mandy. "I

knew I hadn't thought of it! Mom! James! You know what? Oh, we've been so silly, and all because of Jessica!"

Dr. Emily and James stared hard at Mandy. What on earth was she talking about?

"We just assumed that Kimble was her owner's last name because of Jessica Kimble," Mandy said. "But it isn't, is it, girl? It's *your* name. You're named Kimble, aren't you!"

The golden retriever gave one quick, sharp bark. Kimble it was!

Five

"I'm afraid you're right, Mandy." Dr. Emily sighed as she stroked the excited-looking dog. "All right, calm down. That's right, you go and have a drink of water."

"What do you mean, Mom, you're *afraid* I'm right?" Mandy asked. "I think it's fantastic that we know her real name."

"I know what you mean, Dr. Emily," said James. "It's good for Kimble but not so good for us. We're right back to square one. There's no way we can trace her owner now."

Mandy looked crestfallen. She'd been so happy when

the golden retriever had reacted to hearing her real name, she hadn't thought about the rest of it. But maybe they weren't back to square one.

"I'm not so sure, James," she said after a while. "We can tell the SPCA and the police that she's named Kimble. If she's been reported missing her owner would have given the dog's name, too!"

"That's a good point, Mandy. I'll call them now." Dr. Emily ruffled Mandy's hair.

"And it *is* good that we can call Kimble by her real name," said James. "That could help her settle down better."

Mandy nodded. "As soon as Mom's finished on the phone we'll get the box fixed up for her."

The box was just over a square yard. It had a floor but no top. The section at the front was lower and hinged so it could be pulled down. Dr. Emily sent Mandy and James through to the clinic to get a pile of newspapers for lining the floor of the box.

"Because her pups are almost due, we won't give her a blanket or a sheet to lie on," said Dr. Emily. "A little while before she goes into labor, she'll probably want to make a nest and will start looking for something to tear up. So if the newspapers are there, ready for her, she won't get anxious wondering what to use."

"You look busy," came a voice from the doorway.

Mandy looked up with a smile. "Hi, Dad!" she said. "Is Yindee okay?"

"She managed to open the closet door this time," Dr. Adam told them. "She'd chewed a hole about this size" — he made a circle with his thumb and index finger — "in one of Mrs. Anderson's best Yorkshire wool blankets. I can never be sure if it's eating the wool that upsets the cat's stomach or feeling guilty for what she's done. Mrs. Anderson swears Yindee knows when she's been naughty!" Mandy and James laughed.

"It's possible it's some sort of vitamin or mineral deficiency that makes her feel the need to eat wool," Dr. Adam continued. "More than likely it's just a habit, but it's good to check. I've made an appointment for tomorrow. We'll run a couple of tests. What's new with Goldie? Anything?"

Mandy ran over to give him a hug and to tell him the news about the dog's name.

"So it's Kimble, huh?" said Dr. Adam looking across at the golden retriever. "No doubt about that," he added, laughing, as Kimble thumped her tail on the floor.

"Come and look at the box!" Mandy dragged her father to the table. "James did all the assembling," she said. "We're going to put it in its place now that we've lined it."

"The newspaper will be warm for the pups to lie on, won't it?" asked James as he and Dr. Adam lifted the box off the table. "*And* easy to change when it gets soiled."

Dr. Adam nodded. "Yes! Warmth is very important," he said. "If we weren't putting the box in such a cozy place, we would have had to cover the open top with a square of wood and a thick blanket, or use a heat lamp. We'll still have to keep checking on the temperature, but I'm almost sure it will be okay without any of that."

"What should the temperature be, Dr. Adam?" asked James; he was always eager to learn.

"Seventy degrees is the ideal, James. It very rarely falls below that in here at this time of year with the stove going."

The Hopes didn't use the stove very much during the summer months, as it made the kitchen much too hot. Instead, they used the microwave. Mandy, though, was always pleased when the time came to relight the big, friendly stove. She especially loved the coziness of their kitchen in winter.

As soon as Dr. Adam and James moved back from the box, Kimble walked over eagerly. Without hesitation, she stepped over the low front part to settle herself on the bed of newspapers.

"Do you think she might have had a bed like this at home?" James asked.

"Yes, I think that could be the case." Dr. Adam stroked his beard thoughtfully.

Mandy looked at him. "There really is something strange about the whole thing, Dad!" she said. "Kimble's obviously been very well looked after. She seems to be used to lots of love and attention, and it looks as though she's been used to this kind of box."

"Which means her owner must have been preparing for the birth," James added. "I can't believe such a caring owner would abandon her."

"But if she was stolen you'd think we'd have heard from her owner by now." Mandy nodded. "There was that phone call to make sure we'd found her," she said. "That was strange. If it was her owner, it's a shame she didn't tell you what Kimble likes to eat, Dad! I know you said not to worry about her not eating, but maybe she just doesn't like what we're giving her."

"I stopped at Grandma's on my way home," Dr. Adam told her. "She was making stew so I've brought a few chunks of meat home to chop up. Kimble may well be used to some raw meat in her diet. We'll give it to her in a while, but first we'll leave her alone until she's settled in her box. Meanwhile, *I'd* eat almost anything that was offered!"

"Oh, no!" gasped James. "I hadn't realized it was so late. I'll have to go, Mandy. Dad and I are going swimming this afternoon, then we're going to visit my aunt. Will you leave a message with Mom if there's any news about Kimble?"

"Of course I will," Mandy promised. "But you're not staying at your aunt's, are you, James?" she added anxiously. James sometimes spent a couple of days with his cousins during school vacations.

"Not this time," said James.

"So you'll be able to come tomorrow morning?"

James grinned. "Nothing could keep me away!" he said.

That's okay then, thought Mandy as she closed the door behind him. *There's something important James and I need to talk about.*

Kimble stayed happily in her box for an hour or so. Then she got out and walked over to Mandy. She lay her head on Mandy's knee and wagged her tail.

"Are you trying to tell me something?" Mandy asked as she played gently with Kimble's soft golden ears. "Are you hungry? Should we try some of the meat that Dad got for you?"

Mandy mixed the raw meat with a small portion of canned food. She decided not to bother adding anything else. If Kimble ate this meal she'd try adding dry food to the same mix next time.

Kimble ate about half of what Mandy gave her before going to the door and whining to go out.

Dr. Emily was in the garden planting some tulip bulbs. She smiled when Mandy told her that Kimble had eaten a little bit, then suggested that Kimble might like a slow, short walk down the back path. "Put her leash on though, Mandy, and if she shows any reluctance to walk, bring her right back."

"I'll turn back well before we reach the houses anyway," said Mandy. "She might get overexcited if we meet any of the other animals. We don't want her getting into a fight with Tom!"

Walter Pickard lived in one of the houses behind the Fox and Goose and he had three cats. The two females, Scraps and Missie, were friendly, gentle creatures, but Tom was big and fierce and thought nothing of taking on any cat or dog he saw.

"Yes, it wouldn't be good for Tom to set eyes on her," Dr. Emily agreed.

Both Mandy and Kimble enjoyed their short walk. October had been a mild month; the trees were still dressed in their glorious autumnal leaves of yellow, orange, russet, copper, and crimson. The little green flowers were still blossoming on ivy hedges and Mandy saw a blackberry bush still full of juicy berries. Perhaps she'd come and pick some for Grandma after she'd taken Kimble back.

Kimble didn't seem in any hurry to turn back. She was ambling happily along, pausing every now and then to sniff and scratch in the hedges' undergrowth, her tail moving slowly from side to side.

Watching her, Mandy grew thoughtful again. Who could possibly have left her at the door of Animal Ark, and why? "I'll find out, Kimble," she promised aloud. "I don't know how yet, but James and I will think of some way to do it."

Six

Mandy and Kimble were in the backyard when James arrived the next day. He saw them from over the gate. Mandy had let Kimble off the leash and she was walking slowly along the edge of the flower bed, sniffing and scratching at every plant and, now and then, whining anxiously.

"Hello, Kimble," called James. But Kimble didn't even glance toward him. She was too intent on what she was doing.

"You don't look very happy about things, Mandy! Kimble's still okay, isn't she? Your parents haven't changed their minds about her staying here, have they?"

Mandy gave him a weak grin. "No, they wouldn't do that. But you're right about me not feeling too happy. Kimble won't settle indoors at all. She'll come in with me, but two minutes later she'll be scratching at the door to come out here. She's done everything she needs to, so it isn't that."

"Maybe she thinks the box is just for sleeping in. Could she be looking for somewhere to have the pups?" James suggested.

"I wouldn't have thought so," Mandy sighed. "Mom checked her earlier and said she didn't think anything was about to happen just yet. But she does keep whining, so I suppose she might be going into labor."

"Maybe she's pining for her real home and owner, Mandy. She's bound to do that, even with all the love and attention she's getting here. Trouble is, if nobody's called, it looks as though she *has* been abandoned."

"I guess," Mandy nodded. "I want to talk to you about that, but I can't concentrate while Kimble's behaving like this. She hasn't made any attempt to get out of the yard. You'd think she would if her mind was on her real home. She just keeps doing that!" Mandy sighed, and they both gazed to where Kimble was sniffing and scratching.

"Has your mom or dad seen the way she's acting?" James asked.

"No, Mom's been called out and Dad's busy with patients," said Mandy. "And I didn't want to leave her while I went into the clinic."

"I'll go in and see if I can talk to Simon," suggested James. "He might come up with something."

"That's a good idea, James!" Mandy took her eyes off Kimble to smile at him. James turned slightly red and hurried off in the direction of the clinic.

When Kimble reached the far end of the flower bed, she lifted her head and looked around the rest of the yard. After that she turned and made her way over to Mandy. "Do you want to go back indoors?" Mandy asked softly.

Kimble whined, then pawed at Mandy's leggings.

"Oh, Kimble, I really don't know *what* you want," murmured Mandy. The dog moved away and wandered over to the wire run where Mandy's three rabbits played in warm weather. The nights were very cold now so Mandy had moved the hutch into the garage.

Kimble whined, lay down, and tried to get her front paws underneath one of the pieces of wood that supported the wire mesh. There was a small mound of hay in one corner of the run. Kimble seemed to be very interested in it.

Mandy picked the hay up — it was only a handful — and put it between the dog's front paws. Kimble sniffed it, pawed it apart, then looked up at Mandy. She looked bewildered, but all Mandy could do was pet her.

When James came quietly toward them, he was holding a ball, a rubber bone, and a rubber ring.

"Simon thinks she could be searching for something to retrieve!" he said.

"Of course!" Mandy sighed. "Why didn't I think of that! It's in a retriever's nature to pick things up and take them to their owner as presents! I remember reading about it in one of the books we got from the library when we were trying to train Blackie."

James's Labrador was adorable, but he wasn't very obedient. James and Mandy often tried to get him to behave better and had read all sorts of books on dog training.

"Let's put each toy in a different place," said James.

"Okay. I'll hide the ring inside that clump of hay. She seemed extra interested in that," said Mandy.

James didn't hide the bone and the ball; he put them at the edge of the flower bed, a few yards apart. He walked back to Kimble, bent down, and put his arms around her neck. "Go fetch me a present, girl," he whispered into her ear.

One at a time, Kimble fetched the rubber bone, the

ball, and the ring and laid them at Mandy's and James's feet. "Maybe that *was* it!" said James as he petted Kimble's head. "Her tail's really wagging, Mandy."

But the next second, Kimble had returned to the clump of hay. She pawed and sniffed at it, then whined and looked mournfully at Mandy and James.

"I just remembered something else!" cried Mandy. "Wait here, James. And you, too, Kimble."

Mandy came back with an armful of hay. She hurried to the rabbits' run, kicked it carefully with her foot to tilt it on one side, and put the hay down. "Come on, James. We'll wait by the back door," she said.

Once they were there she called, "Okay, Kimble. Find them for me."

"Find what?" James demanded.

"Wait and see," Mandy said, smiling. "I'm sure I've figured it out. Yes . . . yes . . . Look!"

Eyes bright, and her tail wagging really hard, Kimble ambled up the yard toward them. She was holding something in her mouth, but James couldn't see what.

"Hold your hand out, James," whispered Mandy.

James shot Mandy a look, but he did as she'd asked.

"Give it to James. Good girl," Mandy encouraged, and gently and carefully, Kimble deposited an egg in James's hand. She gave a small "wuff," then waddled away back to the hay.

Mandy laughed at the expression on her friend's face. "There was something in one of the books about a golden retriever who used to find and collect duck eggs every day for her owner. Remember?"

"Mandy! That was brilliant!" said James. "Look, here she comes with another egg. How many have you hidden?"

"Six!" Mandy chuckled. "They'll probably still smell newly laid to her," she continued, taking the second egg from Kimble and praising her. "At least, five of them might. Libby Masters brought them this morning."

Libby's family kept free-range hens; the Hopes were among their regular customers.

"I don't suppose Kimble minds if they're newly laid, free-range, or store-bought eggs," said James. "She just seems happy enough to be fetching them."

But that was where James appeared to be wrong. Kimble only brought five eggs and when Mandy went to look, the sixth egg was on the grass and not in the hay where she'd put it. "Kimble found it but she wasn't interested in it!" she called to James.

"Well, she's happy again now," said James, pointing to Kimble. The dog had gone inside and was having a long drink from her water bowl.

"She still isn't very interested in food," said Mandy. "And she's not eager to drink milk, either."

"That dog who collected eggs," said James. "Didn't she like to eat scrambled eggs? I wonder. . . ." He looked thoughtfully at Kimble.

"Good idea, James. I'll go through to the clinic to check with Dad or Simon if it's okay to give her some."

Mandy was almost deafened when she went through the waiting room. Mrs. Anderson had brought Yindee in and the Siamese didn't like being confined in her carrying box.

"Mandy! Am I glad to see you!" Jean Knox had to raise her voice to be heard over the angry yowls. "Simon's helping your father with a dog who isn't too happy about having his wound dressed and that noise is driving us all crazy. Mrs. Anderson says Yindee will settle down all right if we put her in one of our big cages!"

"Okay! I'll take her through to the residential unit." Mandy grinned and grabbed a white coat.

"I'm so sorry about this, Mandy!" said Mrs. Anderson, handing Mandy the carrying box. "Yindee doesn't like being confined in a small space." She looked really embarrassed as Yindee continued to yowl and a couple of dogs started to yap loudly.

"Don't worry. I'll soon have her in a nice big cage," said Mandy.

After washing her hands at the little sink in the unit,

Mandy carefully opened the carrying box and lifted Yindee out. "You really are beautiful, even though you're so noisy," Mandy said. Yindee, her bright blue eyes almost crossed and her brown ears pointing straight up, gave one more yowl and swished her long, dark brown tail from side to side.

When Mandy put Yindee in the cage along with a catnip toy from the carrier, the Siamese gave a tiny meow of approval and began playing with it.

Mandy went back to the waiting area. The door to the exam room opened just then, and a sad-looking basset hound, straining at his leash, almost dragged his owner out. Mandy quickly excused herself from Mrs. Anderson and popped into the exam room to ask her dad about giving Kimble some scrambled eggs.

Dr. Adam said it would be all right and added that he wouldn't mind having some for lunch. So Mandy hurried back to James and the two of them went to work, beating eggs and slicing bread for toast.

"We won't make ours until Mom and Dad come in," said Mandy. "But we could make a small portion now, just for Kimble."

James nodded. "If she eats it, she could have some more when we have ours," he said.

To Mandy's and James's delight, Kimble cleaned her

plate. Then she climbed into her box, plopped herself down, and fell asleep.

"Whew!" sighed Mandy. "This morning was hard work! All that thinking and figuring things out!" She glanced at James and grinned. "But if you agree with what else I've been thinking, we've got a lot more thinking to do!"

"Tell me already!" said James. "You're not making sense."

"Okay. Here goes. You agree that Kimble must have come from a loving home and that her owner obviously cared a lot for her?"

"Definitely!" James nodded hard. "You can tell that by the way she acts. She enjoys being petted and spoken to. I'm sure if a dog wasn't used to that it would take a while for it to respond. I still can't believe that her owner has abandoned her!"

"I think it *was* her owner who abandoned her," said Mandy. "And I don't think it has anything to do with her having pups. But we'll know that when they're born."

"How?" asked James.

"If they're pedigree golden retrievers we'll know for sure," Mandy stated. "Because that would mean the pups' father is a golden retriever, too. He'd have been chosen specially by Kimble's owner."

"Who'd be looking forward to the puppies arriving," said James.

"Exactly!" Mandy nodded. "So *I* think there must be a special reason for Kimble being abandoned, and the only way we'll find out what it is, is by . . ."

"Finding the owner!" James finished for her. "But how, Mandy? How can we do that? The only thing we think we know about her is that she keeps hens or ducks and lets Kimble collect their eggs! And that's not enough to help us!"

"I said we'd have a lot more thinking to —" Mandy broke off abruptly, her eyes growing large as she stared toward Kimble's box.

James spun around. "Oh, no!" he whispered.

Kimble was scratching at the newspaper in her box, tearing it up, and pawing it into a small mound. As James and Mandy watched, she started panting heavily.

"Kimble?" said Mandy in a low voice. Kimble paused in her scratching and glanced up.

"She's got a sort of lost look in her eyes," said James.

Kimble went back to ripping the paper. Her paws were moving faster this time, and suddenly she gave a couple of anxious whines.

"I'm going to get Mom or Dad," said Mandy.

Seven

Mandy dashed out of the kitchen and flew through the door and into the clinic like a whirlwind. "Jean! Is Mom back? Where's Dad?"

"They're in the residential unit," said Jean. The door was swinging shut almost before she'd finished answering.

"Mom! Dad! I think Kimble's getting ready to have her pups! She's panting really hard and ripping up the newspaper. She looks frantic!"

"She's not the only one," Dr. Emily said kindly. "Calm down, honey. There's usually a long time between the dog making a bed for the pups and actually having them."

Dr. Emily's matter-of-fact words calmed Mandy down. She managed a wobbly smile. "I know that, Mom," she said. "I was more or less okay till she whined."

"We'll go and have a look at her," said Dr. Emily, walking to the sink to wash her hands. "I'll leave your dad to settle Morgan down."

"Morgan?" asked Mandy.

Dr. Adam pointed to a cage. "A monster of a mouse with an ingrown claw," he said. "Yindee must have caught his scent. She started hissing and poor Morgan turned into a mass of quivering jelly. He'll be all right. He's hiding in his sleeping quarters."

"I'll come and talk to him later," said Mandy. "Give him some TLC." Mandy's parents often said that her TLC — tender loving care — was as good as medicine.

Dr. Adam nodded and smiled. "That's right, Mandy. Don't keep all your famous TLC for Kimble."

"I think it will be an hour or two at least before anything happens," Dr. Emily told Mandy and James after she'd had a quick look at Kimble. "She's feeling worried and anxious right now. Becoming a mom is a new experience for her."

"What can we do to help her, Dr. Emily?" asked James.

"Just let her go on ripping the newspaper and don't worry about her panting." Dr. Emily smiled. "It's nature's way, James."

"It's the look in her eyes that gets to us, Mom," said Mandy.

"Well, don't let it. What she needs at this stage is gentle sympathy. If you two want to stay with her," Dr. Emily smiled again to soften her words, "she mustn't be encouraged to feel sorry for herself. Understood?"

Mandy and James nodded. "That's okay then," Dr. Emily continued. "And, James, if you want to stay and see the pups being born you'd better check with your parents. It could be a long job."

"Do you mean it, Dr. Emily? Can I really stay?" James's face was flushed with pleasure.

"As long as you and Mandy being here doesn't upset Kimble, yes, you can," she replied. "We'll have lunch now, I think, then I'll probably have time to see to Morgan before Kimble's ready to give birth."

"James and I will make lunch," said Mandy. "It's all ready to cook. Dad said he wanted scrambled eggs."

"Fine. Call us when it's ready. I'll go and see if I can juggle this afternoon's workload around a bit and try to make sure either your dad or I can be on hand. Oh, and if Kimble wants a drink, that's all right, Mandy, but I think water or *cold* milk would be better. Sometimes warm milk can make a dog feel sleepy, and that could deaden her labor pains. Then she might not recognize when it's time for her to bear down to push the puppies out," she explained.

"If Kimble couldn't push would you have to deliver the pups by operating on her, Mom?" asked Mandy.

"Possibly," replied Dr. Emily. "Or sometimes special injections can help. But don't worry about something that probably won't happen. Most dogs manage perfectly well on their own."

"Come on, Mandy. Let's finish making lunch," said James as Dr. Emily left the room. "It will take our minds off Kimble for a while," he added.

Mandy smiled. It was really good that James was here with her.

"Okay," said Mandy when they'd eaten lunch and cleaned up. "We might as well make use of the waiting time, James. Let's make a list of ideas for finding Kimble's owner."

Dr. Emily had checked Kimble again and told them to call her if there was any change, adding that she'd come back in half an hour anyway.

James glanced at the golden retriever. "I know we're not supposed to feel sorry for her," he said. "But it's hard not to, Mandy. She looks so . . . so . . . far away from us."

"I know," Mandy agreed quietly. "I guess a dog having her first litter always looks like that. It's probably worse for Kimble because she's in a strange place. That's why we've got to work on this list!"

"Right!" said James, picking up a pen. "Your parents have contacted all the official authorities, so we've got to think of people who come into contact with dogs in other ways. Like the groomer in Walton!" he said, writing it down. "Jane and Andrew, the owners, don't only groom dogs, they sell pet food. We get Blackie's food from them. They deliver it. They probably cover quite a wide area."

"James, you're brilliant!" said Mandy. "They'll know lots of dogs!"

"So they just *might* know Kimble!" said James. "We could go and see them tomorrow."

Mandy nodded. "And there's the traveling library. Everyone talks to Mrs. Chambers about their dogs and takes them on the van to see her. And she brings her dog to Animal Ark, so we'll have her home number on record."

"Mailmen!" said James. "They know everybody's

dogs. We'll ask our mailman to put a sign up in the post office and see if he'll get other offices to put one up, too! Something like 'Do you know the owner of this dog?' with a description of Kimble underneath."

"And a photograph," said Mandy. "We can get film for Dad's camera when we go into Walton tomorrow."

"Now we're beginning to get somewhere!" said James.

"I think Kimble is, too!" Mandy said softly. "She's squatting, James. She looks as if she's straining a bit. I'll go and get Mom."

Mandy forced herself to walk unhurriedly out of the kitchen and managed to keep calm when she went into the exam room to get Dr. Emily; Jean had warned her that her mother was attending to Morgan. Mandy didn't want to startle either of them.

"All right, Mandy. I've just finished checking on Morgan. He'll feel a lot better now that his claw isn't digging into his pad. You take some of the small towels, packets of rubber gloves, and garbage bags for soiled bedding. And white coats for you and James," she added. "Scrub your hands thoroughly. I'll put Morgan back in his cage and be right with you."

James looked really glad to see Mandy. "Nothing's happening," he said as he put on his white coat. "I was just worried it might."

"I was only gone a couple of minutes," Mandy smiled.

"Yes, well, it seemed like ages," said James, shoving his glasses farther onto the bridge of his nose. "Kimble's looking at us, Mandy. Do you think she wants to be petted, or should we leave her alone?"

"We'll ask Mom when she comes," said Mandy. "She'll be here soon."

"She isn't straining for real yet, but I think she soon will be," said Dr. Emily when she checked Kimble. "I think maybe she would like you close by. Some dogs like being left alone to get on with things, others like someone within reach. Just kneel or sit by the box and see what she does."

Kimble stretched her head out and sniffed first at Mandy's shoulder, then at James's. Then she moved back, circled the box two or three times, and lay down.

"She might feel comfier lying down for the birth," Dr. Emily said quietly.

"She's stuck one paw over the edge of the box," whispered James. "Do you think she wants me to hold it, Dr. Emily?"

"Could be." Dr. Emily nodded. "You can take it in turns, a few minutes at a time. And I think we should get prepared now.

"Warm water, rags, the small towels, and rubber gloves, Mandy, and a cardboard box and heating pad in case we need to separate the pups from Kimble for any reason. Anything else we might need is on my exam tray on the table."

Kimble made a small whimper of protest when, after ten minutes or so, James let go of her paw so Mandy could hold it. "All right, Kimble," Mandy whispered. "I'm here for you now."

A short while later, Kimble's paw jerked, then tensed in Mandy's hand. Mandy turned her head to look up at her mom.

"Well, pup number one is about to arrive, I think," Dr. Emily murmured, her eyes on the dog. "Here it comes," she said.

Then she shook her head. "Kimble doesn't understand what she should be doing. I'll have to show her."

"What is she supposed to be doing?" asked Mandy.

Dr. Emily glanced very briefly at Mandy and James, her eyes soft as she noticed their earnest but worried expressions. "She should be licking the puppy," she said. "Feeling Kimble's tongue would rouse the pup and encourage it to take its first breath. So the important thing," she continued, working as she spoke, "is to tear the membrane over the puppy's nose — pass me a paper towel from my tray, James — then to open its mouth and clear the mucus away with the paper towel and clear its nose as well."

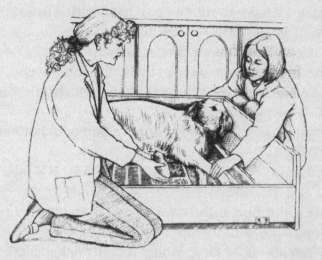

Mandy and James hardly breathed as Dr. Emily held the tiny puppy upside down. "It allows any fluid to drain," she explained; then she smiled as the puppy coughed.

"I'll lay him next to Kimble now and see if she'll take over. There, Kimble, what do you think? Your firstborn is a tiny boy pup. Let go of her paw now, Mandy," said Dr. Emily without changing the steady and comforting tone of voice.

"What should she do now, Mom?" Mandy used the same soft tone. "Bite off the cord?"

"Yes, then lick the puppy. But I don't think she's going to do it. I'll have to rub the pup hard with a towel. Don't worry if he screams, I want him to. Once Kimble hears him protesting she might take some interest."

The little pup squealed alarmingly; Kimble got to her feet and James and Mandy looked at each other in delight. It was working!

But it wasn't! Kimble lay down again with her back to them.

"All right, not to worry," said Dr. Emily. "I'll take care of it."

"We'll put him in the cardboard box with the heating pad and a layer of towels," she said.

"What about feeding, Mom?" Mandy asked anxiously. "Isn't it important for him to have some milk as soon as possible?"

"It is, but we mustn't force the puppy on her. Not just yet," said Dr. Emily. "When the second pup arrives, Kimble might react differently. She might deal with everything herself. Then we can put both pups to suckle at the same time."

The second puppy was born twenty minutes later. Kimble put her nose close but again she didn't attempt to tear the sac.

"Do you want to do it, Mandy?"

Mandy took a deep breath and nodded. She could

hardly believe her mother was trusting her to do such an important job.

"Okay. Make sure Kimble can see what you're doing . . . use your thumbnail to break the membrane over the pup's nose . . . that's it. Open its mouth and" — Dr. Emily passed her daughter a paper towel — "clear the mucus away. And from the nostrils, that's right."

"Now do I hold the pup's head down?" asked Mandy, and her mother nodded. The tiny creature didn't cough, though. It appeared to be lifeless.

"I'll take over." Dr. Emily took the pup and gently but firmly tapped its rear end. Nothing happened and Mandy heard James swallowing hard.

"This looks cruel," Dr. Emily warned them. "But it sometimes works . . ." And, holding the pup by its back legs, she swung it from side to side.

Mandy bit hard on her lip and James knelt upright, his body rigid, his glasses slipping down his nose. But just then the pup made a noise like a strangled sneeze. They both felt like cheering!

Dr. Emily smiled her relief and Kimble got to her feet and nosed at Dr. Emily's hand. "She wants it!" Mandy gasped in delight as the golden retriever licked the pup from head to tail. "This time she really does want it. Is it a girl or a boy, Mom?"

"A girl," said Dr. Emily.

Suddenly, the puppy squealed and squealed; James and Mandy looked into the box, then, in alarm, at Dr. Emily. She laughed at the expression on their faces. "It's all right, Kimble's not eating the pup. She's bitten the cord off. That often makes a pup yell."

James took his glasses off and rubbed them on his white coat. "Whew!" He grinned. "This is a real nail-biting experience."

"The pup needs rubbing with a towel," said Dr. Emily. "Do you think you're up to it, James?"

James's glasses were back in place in a flash. He took the towel from Dr. Emily, knelt over the box, and whispered, "Don't worry, Kimble. I'm just going to finish drying your pup. I'll put her back in a minute, I promise."

Kimble watched James with huge anxious eyes and Dr. Emily smiled in satisfaction. "Hold on a second before you put her back, James." She reached into the cardboard box for the firstborn pup. "Her maternal instinct seems quite strong now. We'll put both puppies to suckle together. Ready, James? Here we go."

Kimble nosed halfheartedly at the boy pup, then turned all her attention to the second one. "She's not too keen on the poor guy, but at least she's letting him feed," said Dr. Emily. "Pour some milk, Mandy. We'll leave them for a few minutes, then see if Kimble will have a drink herself. Then we'll change the newspapers."

Kimble lapped eagerly at the cold milk. "It's the first time she's really seemed to enjoy it," James commented.

"Are we leaving the puppies in with her while the rest are being born, Mom?"

"Maybe. We'll wait and see. If Kimble gets too restless or there are any problems, we'll move them. She's settling herself down, so I think it will be a while before any more arrive. And unless she shows signs of needing us, we'll leave her alone."

Dr. Emily passed through to the clinic to check that everything was running smoothly. It was time for afternoon office hours; Animal Ark was busy, but her husband and Simon were coping.

James and Mandy made themselves milk shakes and sandwiches and sat at the table to discuss their plans for the following day. They decided they'd go to the post office and ask about putting a sign up. It would be easier than trying to catch their own mailman. After that they'd bike into Walton, buy film for the camera, then stop in at the groomer.

"We can ask the owners if they know anyone with a golden retriever who might be the father," Mandy suggested. "I think the pups could be pedigrees."

"It's hard to tell when they're such tiny things and their eyes are closed and their ears are so close to their heads," said James.

"You're right." Mandy nodded but she was more convinced than ever that Kimble's owner had planned for the pups.

She got up to take their used dishes to the sink, glancing into the box as she went past. "James," she whispered urgently. "Kimble's had another pup. She knows what to do now."

"It's very still," James said dubiously. "Do you think it needs shaking like the other one did?"

Mandy heard the door open and turned in relief. "Mom! There's a third puppy and it isn't moving."

Dr. Emily hurried to the box and lifted the pup. She stared at it for a long second, then lifted her eyes to Mandy and James. Mandy's face clouded over. She knew immediately what her mother was going to say.

Eight

"This little one didn't make it, I'm afraid," Dr. Emily said. She spoke briskly but her green eyes were soft and sympathetic.

"It's a shame it had to happen just as Kimble had learned how to do everything all by herself," said Mandy in a choked voice.

Her mother nodded and turned her attention to Kimble. "She's all right," she said a few minutes later.

"And she's getting out of her box, Mom! Is that because she doesn't want to know the other pups now?"

"She might feel the need to exercise," said Dr. Emily. "Some dogs like a little walk around in between pups arriving. She's going to the door, Mandy. Put her collar and leash on and take her into the yard. Only stay out a minute, though. It's cold outside. I'll stop by the clinic while you're gone."

Mandy nodded and blinked. She guessed her mom was going to take the dead puppy out of the way. "Coming, James?" she asked.

To her surprise, James gave her arm a quick squeeze as she opened the door. "There's still the first two, Mandy," he said. "And however many more she has. They'll be all right, just you wait and see."

"You're right, James. I'll think positively!" said Mandy. And as they let Kimble walk slowly around the yard, she thought what a good friend James was.

When they went back inside, Kimble wandered over to her water bowl; Mandy and James waited anxiously to see if she'd go to her box when she'd had a drink.

"It's okay, she's going," said Mandy. They watched Kimble climb in and settle herself down close to the two pups. She licked the girl pup and ignored the boy.

"She doesn't seem to like him at all," Mandy said sadly. "Poor little . . ." She glanced at James. "They ought to have names," she added.

"How about Jake?" said James, his eyes on the boy pup.

"That was quick!" said Mandy.

James nodded. "I was thinking about it when we took Kimble outside," he said. "Do you like it?"

"Yes, it sounds just right," said Mandy. "What do you think of Pippa for his sister?"

"That sounds just right, too," James replied with a grin.

'There's a strong possibility we'll have to help rear Jake," said Dr. Emily after she'd returned and put him to suckle. "Good girl, Kimble, let him feed. That's right. Good dog."

An hour went by before Kimble showed signs of having another puppy. She started getting restless, standing up, then circling around. "Let's move Pippa and Jake into the other box, Mandy," said her mom. "I know you'd both love to cuddle them, but it's best to handle them as little as possible."

Mandy and James nodded, then quickly but carefully each picked up a pup and laid the tiny bundles side by side in the heated box.

Kimble didn't have any trouble delivering the next pup but she didn't attempt to tear the sac; she didn't even look at it.

"This one's a boy," said Dr. Emily, working quickly. "He's small and weak. I think we'll have a fight on our hands to save him."

"Felix?" Mandy asked James. "Shall we call him Felix?"

"Okay," said James. Then he burst out, "Kimble looks so sad and confused, I hope there aren't too many more pups."

Dr. Emily was examining Kimble. She glanced up at James. "Don't worry too much about her, James," she said. "Dogs do sometimes react like this when it's their first litter. She'll probably feel happier about things in a day or two. And I can't feel any more pups. I think Felix was the last one."

A little while later, Kimble let Dr. Emily help Felix to feed from her but showed no interest in him at all.

Mandy sighed. "Would Kimble be acting differently toward her babies if she were with her owner, Mom?"

Dr. Emily nodded. "Possibly. I'm going to check her over again and change the bedding, then we'll leave her in peace and quiet. She might come around to accepting them wholeheartedly in an hour or so. Meanwhile, Mandy, I think your dad would appreciate a hand in cleaning up after office hours."

"I'd better be going," said James. "Blackie hasn't seen me today. He'll be sulking."

"So will my rabbits," said Mandy. "I'll go and see to them first, Mom, before I go and do my chores in the clinic."

Playing with her rabbits, feeding them, and settling them down for the night soothed Mandy a little bit. And scrubbing and disinfecting the exam tables and counter-tops, mopping the floors, and tidying the waiting area helped, too.

After a while, Dr. Adam joined Mandy in the residential unit. "Better now?" he asked, ruffling her hair.

Mandy nodded. "A little bit. I know I shouldn't get so upset when things go wrong. Kimble's got two healthy puppies and the little one *might* make it. I just wish she would show more interest in them. I'm sure she would if she was in her own home. But James and I are going to try to do something about that!" she added determinedly.

"That's my girl," laughed Dr. Adam. "I'm sure if anyone can do anything, you and James can. Now, Mom wants us to take feeding bottles and some feeding formula with us." Mandy knew that the formula was especially for hand-rearing. It was as close as possible to the mother's milk, containing everything a puppy needed.

"The tiniest pup is too weak to suckle from Kimble, so he's going to need extra feeding and a lot of attention," Dr. Adam continued. "You can be on duty till midnight, then Mom or I will take over. Okay?"

"Okay!" Mandy agreed.

*   *   *

It was hard work trying to coax the tiny puppy to feed from the banana-shaped feeding bottle. Dr. Adam had enlarged the holes so Felix wouldn't have to suck too hard. But he only took a little bit before falling asleep.

"If that's all he'll take at a time, we'll have to feed him hourly," said Dr. Adam. He stroked his beard and looked at Mandy, his eyes serious.

"I know, Dad," Mandy sighed sadly. "We'll be lucky if he survives. I'm not giving up on him yet, though!"

Mandy tried flicking Felix's back paws gently to wake

him but it didn't work; so she rubbed all around his abdomen with a warm wet piece of cotton to help him digest the milk formula.

"Shall I put him in with Kimble and the other two, Dad?" she asked.

"Yes. Although she isn't taking any notice of him, she does let him lie close," said Dr. Emily. "Snuggling up to her and his brother and sister will give him comfort and help to keep him warm."

Kimble raised her head to gaze at Mandy when she placed Felix in between the other two. Mandy felt her heart lurch. Kimble looked more forlorn than she ever had before. "Is she just tired out, Dad?" she whispered, stroking the dog's big golden head.

"There's more to it than that," Dr. Adam replied. "I think she's missing her home and her owner more than ever. She's okay physically at the moment, but the birth dehydrated her and I'd feel a lot happier if she'd drink more. You could try giving her some lukewarm milk, Mandy. I'm going to help your mom with some paperwork now. Call us if you need us."

By midnight, Mandy could hardly keep her eyes open. She'd managed to persuade Kimble to drink a little and she'd fed Felix another three times. He hadn't drunk much, but at least he'd had some. Kimble had suckled the other two pups. She'd licked and cleaned Pippa each time but ignored the boy pup. So Mandy had rubbed Jake with warm wet cotton and he seemed to be okay.

Dr. Emily had said good night some time earlier. "Dad's doing first shift. I'll come down at three o'clock," she'd told Mandy after hearing the progress report and checking Kimble and the pups.

When Dr. Adam arrived to take over from Mandy, she had just made some cocoa. "I'll take mine up with me," she said, walking over to have one last look at Kimble and the puppies.

Suddenly, Kimble jumped to her feet. She got out of the box and stood looking at Mandy. Then she whined!

"What's wrong, sweetheart?" asked Mandy, bending low to pet the dog.

Kimble raised her head and sniffed; then she tried to reach Mandy's mug. "Do you want some cocoa?" said Mandy. "Is that it? Sorry, girl, but that's not good for you."

"Let's try some milk, instead," Dr. Adam said. He poured some in Kimble's bowl. Mandy smiled at her dad as Kimble halfheartedly lapped at the milk. Feeling a little happier about Kimble, Mandy took her cocoa and went up to bed.

"But your parents do think Jake and Pippa will be okay?" James said. He and Mandy were on their way to the post office and Mandy had given him a full report on Kimble and her family.

Felix was still alive but it was a real effort to get him to feed and Mandy knew there wasn't much hope for him.

Mandy nodded. "Even though Kimble won't have much to do with Jake, she lets him feed. One of us has to clean him and rub him to help him digest the milk, though. She's not overly loving toward Pippa, either, but she *is* looking after her. We've just *got* to find her owner, James. I'm sure she'd be a great mom if she wasn't pining so much!"

The man Mandy and James were told to speak to at the post office seemed unfriendly; Mandy's heart sank when he asked them brusquely what they wanted. She gave him her best smile and explained the situation as briefly as possible.

"Anyone who'd do a thing like that isn't worth being found!" he snapped. "Surely, if the poor dog had been stolen, the owner could have traced her by now." He gazed thoughtfully at Mandy, then, to her astonishment, said, "I'd give her the sort of home she deserves. My old dog was sixteen when she died. I'd had her since she was a pup. You don't get over losing a good friend and companion that quickly. But it was almost a year ago now."

"Yes, but . . ." Mandy bit her lip and glanced at James for help. He took over briskly and efficiently.

"Kimble's pining badly," he said. "For her sake, and the puppies' sake, it's worth trying to find the owner. We're sure Kimble came from a very caring and loving home, and we need to find out what happened to make the owner abandon her."

"All right. You win. You can bring some signs. I'll put a couple up here and I'll circulate some to other post offices. That is" — he held a hand up to stem Mandy's flow of thanks — "as long as you guarantee that if the owner comes forward, he or she will be questioned thoroughly before being allowed to have the dog back."

"If and when we find the owner, the SPCA will take over," Mandy told him.

"Fine. That's fine. I'd like you to make it clear on the sign that's what will happen. Perhaps you'd better ask anyone who has any information to get in touch with their local SPCA."

James nodded. "We'll do that," he said.

"Good. And make it known that I'd be willing to give the girl a loving home if nobody claims her. Now go ahead and get those signs done. I'll expect you back first thing tomorrow. And just make sure you get good photos of the dog. We don't want any cases of mistaken identity."

"I thought we were going to have a big problem with him at first," said Mandy as they biked off. "But he's nice under that gruff manner."

James smiled. Anyone who cared about dogs was okay as far as he was concerned. "You do realize we'll have to go and buy the film, come straight home and take the photos, then go back into Walton to get them developed?" he asked.

Mandy glanced questioningly at him.

"Otherwise," James pointed out, "we won't have the photos in time to take the signs to the post office tomorrow morning. If we don't take them then, he's likely to change his mind."

"It's no problem, really," said Mandy. "Apart from making the trip twice," she added with a grin. The road to Walton was a hilly one. "Then," she continued, "we can stop at the groomer while we're waiting for the film to be developed."

When they got back to Animal Ark, Mandy made up some milk formula to feed Felix, while James took photos of Kimble. Dr. Adam's camera was easy to use; it automatically adjusted itself, so James didn't have to worry about getting the pictures in focus.

"He's all skin and bones, Dad!" sighed Mandy as she cradled Felix in the palm of her hand. "He won't lick my finger when I run it around his mouth, and I've put a tiny drop of milk on his nose, but he isn't wrinkling it or anything! He's just lying here helpless, and I can't help him!"

"The little fellow's getting weaker," said Dr. Adam as he watched Mandy gently squeezing the corners of the pup's mouth, trying to help him suck at the bottle. "I'll go and get a syringe. We might be able to dribble a drop of milk into his mouth with that."

Dr. Adam returned, emptied the milk from the bottle into the small plastic container he'd brought as well, then filled the syringe a little.

"Okay, put your hand under his chin to support it. I'll see what I can do."

Mandy watched hopefully as her dad held the end of the syringe that looked like a miniature plastic straw against one corner of Felix's mouth. "Is it easier for him to swallow if the milk goes in through the side of his mouth?" Mandy asked.

Dr. Adam nodded. "This tiny tube is at a slight angle, pointing toward the back of Felix's throat," he said. "So as long as I don't press the plunger too hard and release too much at once, there's less chance of the milk just trickling straight out again."

"He swallowed, Dad. I felt his throat move," said Mandy.

But when Dr. Adam carefully released another drop of milk it trickled back out almost right away.

"Poor little Felix," whispered Mandy as she dabbed gently at his mouth with some cotton. She gave a deep, sad sigh and looked across at James. "Take a photo of him, James," she said huskily. "When we find Kimble's owner we'll at least be able to show her a picture of the youngest pup."

Dr. Adam nodded and squeezed her shoulder. "I think the other two will make it through all right," he said. "We can't win every time, you know. No matter how hard we try."

"I know, Dad. It still hurts, though! Still, there are all the other animals to think of." Mandy gave him a wobbly smile. "What's new in the clinic. Any admissions?"

"Yes. One of Johnny Foster's guinea pigs. It had a nasty splinter in its cheek. Simon got the splinter out, but we're keeping Brandy in overnight to make sure there's no infection. Morgan the monster mouse is going home later, and your mom is taking blood samples from Yindee right now."

"Did Libby bring any more eggs?" asked Mandy after she'd put Felix into his heated box. "Kimble's going toward the back door. If she wants to go out it might cheer her up if we hid a couple in the hay for her to retrieve."

"Yes, they're in the pantry," said Dr. Adam. "We'll make some scrambled eggs for Kimble to eat. She needs some nourishment. She's not had much to drink."

So Mandy got two eggs and hid them in the hay. Kimble collected them when Mandy asked her to. But she didn't wag her tail either time when she dropped them into Mandy's hand.

James watched with a sad look on his face. Then he said abruptly, "I can't bear to see her like this. We've *got* to find her owner. Let's get this film back to the photo shop, Mandy. The sooner we do that and get to the groomer, the better!"

Nine

At the groomer neither Jane nor Andrew, the two owners, recognized the description of Kimble. "We don't have many golden retrievers in for grooming," said Jane, who was busy clipping a black poodle. "We deliver pet food to one house where there's one. He's won lots of prizes and he's fathered quite a few litters. But he's getting older now; I don't think he could be the father."

"We'll ask his owner if she's ever seen a dog like Kimble at any of the shows," said Andrew. "I know she still goes to them, even though she doesn't enter her dog anymore. If you let us have a photo, we'll show it to her and anyone else we can think of."

Mandy smiled and asked Andrew if it would be okay to pet the dog he was combing out.

"He's terrific, isn't he?" said James. "I always think chows look so dignified."

"He's named Leo," Andrew told them. "It suits him, doesn't it? He does look like a lion."

"Does he live around here?" asked Mandy. "I've never seen him before. He doesn't come to Animal Ark."

"He lives in Sheffield but his owner works in Walton and brings him in once a month," said Andrew. "He likes you, Mandy," he added as Leo licked Mandy's hand. "Would you like to finish combing him out?"

"We need to come back here anyway with some photos," said James when Mandy hesitated. "You stay here and groom Leo while I go to the photo shop."

"So," Mandy said to her parents a couple of hours later, "Jane and Andrew have a photo to show around and James has gone home to make the signs for the post offices."

It was almost time for evening office hours. Dr. Adam and Dr. Emily were having a quick cup of coffee before it started, and Mandy was preparing a meal for Felix as she talked.

"I'll call Mrs. Chambers later," she continued, "and ask her if anyone who uses the library van has a dog like Kimble, and if none of that works, well, I can't think of anything else at the moment!"

"The two of you have certainly come up with some good ideas." Dr. Emily walked over to look at Kimble, who was lying quietly with her puppies. "Let's hope one of them produces a result. Kimble is really down in the dumps."

Dr. Adam nodded. "See if you can persuade her to drink some milk after you've fed the pup, Mandy. If she doesn't start taking more fluids soon we'll have to put her on an intravenous line to prevent dehydration."

"If that happens, would we have to bottle-feed Jake and Pippa, Dad?" Mandy asked.

"We may have to anyway," Dr. Adam replied. "I've got a feeling the poor girl is on the verge of rejecting them completely."

When her parents had gone through to the clinic, Mandy sighed and looked sadly down at Kimble. Then she shook her head. *I can't let her see I'm worried*, she thought. *It might make her worse.*

Mandy tried to keep calm and cheerful but it was hard work; the tiniest pup hadn't taken much milk and Kimble moved out of the box when the other two started suckling from her.

"I bet you're thirsty, Kimble," Mandy said encouragingly. "Let's have some milk, okay?"

Kimble was lapping halfheartedly at her milk when there was knocking on the back door. Mandy hurried to open it and Elise Knight dashed in with Jet in her arms and Maisy walking behind.

"I came the back way because it's quicker," she gasped. "Jet's swallowed one of my pearl earrings, Mandy! It was my fault. She knocked it off the dresser and started playing with it. When she picked it up I tried to get it out of her mouth. But she swallowed it. I'm so scared it will get stuck somewhere inside her."

"How big's the earring?" asked Mandy, taking the black cat from Elise.

"I brought the other one." Elise gave it to Mandy.

"Okay, I'll take her through to the clinic," said Mandy. "Don't worry, Elise, it's not a very big pearl."

When Mandy returned to the kitchen, she smiled reassuringly at Elise. "Mom says not to worry, she'll give Jet some castor oil. She says leave her with us for tonight, though, and —" Mandy broke off with a gasp as she noticed what Maisy was doing.

The dalmatian was sitting close to the box, staring down intently, her head tilted to one side. "She's looking at the puppies!"

"Puppies?" Elise asked. "Whose?"

"Kimble's." Mandy pointed to the golden retriever. Kimble was lying down by her bowl, her big head resting on her front paws as she gazed mournfully into space.

"I was so worried about Jet I didn't even see her," said Elise. "What's wrong with her, Mandy? She looks so sad!" Then she added urgently, "Maisy's got her head right in the puppies' box! Kimble won't like that! She might go for her."

"I don't think she will," said Mandy. "She's too sad to bother. But I'll keep an eye on her while you get Maisy."

"Okay!" Elise took a couple of steps forward, then paused. "Maisy's licking the puppies," she said, glancing across at Mandy.

Mandy nodded. "Just take it nice and slow," she replied quietly. She knew Elise was trying to figure out the best way of moving the deaf dog without making her jump.

But before Elise had time to move again, one of the pups squeaked.

Kimble was on her feet and at the box in a flash, the instinct to protect her litter suddenly strongly aroused in her. She barged into Maisy, pushing her away, and climbed into the box.

Elise took hold of Maisy's collar and Mandy froze and held her breath.

Then she said, "Kimble's licking them. *All* of them!" Half laughing and half crying, she watched Kimble's

pink tongue working its way over the pups' squirming
bodies. Even tiny Felix was squirming a little. One
of them was whimpering with pleasure but Mandy
couldn't tell which it was. She didn't dare go too near.

Maisy's tail was wagging and it brushed against
Mandy's leg. "Oh, Maisy!" Mandy knelt down and held
the dalmatian's head in her hands. "You're a good, good
girl. You've made Kimble realize that she does love her
puppies after all!"

Elise shook her head in bewilderment. Mandy grinned, then told her the whole story. "So if you hadn't had to bring in Jet, Maisy wouldn't have seen the pups and Kimble wouldn't be loving them like she is now!"

Mandy glanced again toward the box. Kimble was letting Jake and Pippa feed while she licked Felix. "We're not sure that one is going to make it," she said sadly, "but at least he'll have had some love from his mother!"

"Oh, Mandy!" Elise gave her a quick, firm hug and wiped away a tear.

Dr. Adam came in a few minutes later to tell Elise that Jet had been given a dose of castor oil, and all being well, Elise would be able to take her home first thing in the morning.

"Should I go and see her or not?" Elise asked him. "I don't want to upset her."

"I would leave her," advised Dr. Adam. "She's in a cage next to Yindee. They're 'talking' away to each other. A fine pair they are," he said. "A wool-eater and a pearl-eater. Yindee's test results are all okay," he added to Mandy. "So I guess the wool-eating is just a habit!"

"Let's hope she doesn't give Jet any ideas then," chuckled Mandy.

"You look as happy as a clam, Mandy," he said, noticing Mandy's smile.

Mandy nodded and told him what had happened. Maisy woofed with delight when Dr. Adam took her head in his hands to praise her. "We'll send for you if Kimble loses interest in her pups again," he told her, his mouth close to one ear so she could feel the vibration of his voice even though she couldn't hear it.

"Maybe she won't have time to lose interest again," said Elise. "Maybe Mandy and James's efforts to find her owner will pay off quickly."

"Oh, I hope so," sighed Mandy. "Once I've called the librarian and James and I have taken the signs to the post office, we won't be able to do anything but wait!" Mandy was never very good at just waiting for things to happen; she liked to be doing something to help them happen.

Elise and Maisy left and Mandy glanced up at her father. "I was about to feed Felix before all that happened," she said. "Should I try now, Dad, or leave him while Kimble's loving him?"

"Being licked by Kimble could just stimulate him enough to give him the incentive to take some milk," he replied thoughtfully. "But I doubt he's up to suckling yet." He crouched down and spoke softly to Kimble as he stroked Felix with one finger. Kimble didn't stop licking the pup but she wagged her tail and didn't try to nudge Dr. Adam's finger away.

"I don't think Kimble would mind if you tried feeding him from the syringe while she's licking him," he said.

So Mandy half filled the syringe and knelt down by the box. "Is this okay, girl?" she asked Kimble. "Can I try to feed your pup? There, I'll put one hand under his front paws so I can hold his head up a bit with my thumb. That's right, you lick his stomach. Now I'm going to put this in his mouth. It's got milk in it, see?"

Kimble gave a small whine, then licked Mandy's hand before returning her attention to licking Felix's stomach.

"It's working, Dad!" Mandy whispered after a while. "I felt his little throat move when he swallowed. That's it, Felix. Swallow again, and again. His tongue's moving now! He's getting the idea, Dad. He's taking quite a bit. And now he's wrinkling his nose. Whoops!"

Mandy chuckled as Felix sneezed. Kimble pushed Mandy's hand away with her paw, then sniffed anxiously around the pup's mouth and nose. "He's all right, Kimble. I haven't hurt him," Mandy assured her.

Kimble sniffed and licked for a while. Then she scooped Felix along with one paw and tucked him firmly against her stomach next to Pippa and Jake.

"She's telling me that it's time for Felix to sleep," said Mandy. "I'll give him some more in an hour or so. Kimble looks a bit happier now, doesn't she? But she's still got that sort of questioning look in her eyes. As if she's wondering what she's doing here."

Dr. Adam nodded. "I'm almost sure the pups are pedigreed goldens," he said. "So that makes it likely that Kimble was abandoned for a reason other than her being pregnant."

"We've got to try to find out what that reason was!" said Mandy. "Oh, I still haven't called Mrs. Chambers." She glanced at the clock. "I'll do that now. She should be home from her library rounds."

"Remember, Mandy," said Dr. Adam, "*if* Kimble's owner is traced, it will be the start of another long haul."

"At least we'd have something else to start *on*!" said Mandy. "Okay, I know," she added, catching her dad's warning glance. "It'll be up to the SPCA. But you never know, they might need a bit of help."

Ten

Mandy dashed downstairs, brushing her hair as she went. She'd overslept and she and James had arranged to meet early to take the signs to the post office. They were going to walk there and take Blackie with them.

I'll have to feed Felix first, though, she thought, hurtling into the kitchen.

"Morning, Mom. Morning, Dad," she said, walking toward the box.

"Hang on a minute, Mandy," Dr. Emily said quietly.

Mandy stopped dead. Her heart sank as she saw the

look on her mom's face. "What's up?" she whispered. "Something's happened, hasn't it?"

Dr. Emily nodded. "Yes, it's bad news, honey," she said. "I'm afraid Felix died about an hour ago."

"Oh, Mom!" Mandy walked slowly to the table and sat down. "I know we didn't expect him to make it at first," she said. "But then when Kimble started mothering him properly and he started taking some milk —" Mandy felt like her heart was breaking. Anguished, she turned to look at her mom.

"He took a lot from the syringe every time I fed him last night. He even —" Mandy gulped and dashed her hand across her eyes before she continued. "He licked my fingers, Mom. He seemed to be getting stronger. I thought he had a chance. What happened? Why did he die? Would it have made any difference if Kimble had taken to him right away?"

"I don't think it would have mattered, Mandy," said Dr. Adam. "He was just too weak. If he had lived, I doubt he'd have been able to lead the active sort of life a retriever should. Sometimes, hard though it seems, nature does know best."

Mandy nodded. She knew her dad wasn't saying that just to try to make her feel better. Her parents were always honest with her. "It still hurts when it happens though," she said. She looked at her mother. "He wasn't — did he feel anything, Mom? Was he in pain?"

Dr. Emily's green eyes were misty when she replied, "He died peacefully, Mandy." She reached across the table to give Mandy's hand a quick squeeze. "He was snuggled up to Kimble. I think she sensed what was about to happen. She was licking him very slowly and gently. One second he was breathing and the next second he wasn't."

"What did Kimble do when it happened?" Mandy asked, her eyes wide. "Do you think she was upset, Mom?"

"That's the next thing," Dr. Emily said. "Kimble is rather distressed. No," she added quickly, "don't go to her, Mandy. She's feeling a bit overprotective of the other two pups at the moment."

"She growls if we go near," said Dr. Adam. "So we're best just leaving her completely alone."

"Is that something to worry about?" asked Mandy. "Or is it good that she's feeling protective?"

"It could be something to worry about." Dr. Adam nodded. "She wasn't really eating or drinking enough before. Now she might refuse to leave her puppies at all. And if she doesn't like us going near her box, she might not eat or drink from a bowl we put in it. A protective mother dog sometimes loses trust even in people she knows well."

"And she'll see us as strangers more than ever now," Mandy said sadly.

"But thanks to Maisy, at least Kimble cares about the pups now," said Dr. Adam. "It could be that instinct will tell her to take nourishment so she can keep feeding them. We'll just have to wait and see."

Mandy sighed. "It's like taking one step forward, then two steps back," she said.

Her parents smiled and Dr. Adam stood up. "Time for me to take some forward steps," he said. "It's my farm rounds today."

"Yes, and if I'm going to be on time to meet James, I'd better have my breakfast, then get started on my chores," said Mandy, reaching for the cereal box.

James and Blackie were already waiting at the Fox and Goose crossroads. Blackie greeted Mandy with enthusiasm. She cuddled and petted him while she broke the sad news to James about Felix.

"Well, if your parents think it was for the best, then I'm sure it was," said James. "We've just got to do our very best for Kimble now."

Mandy gave him a quick smile, then gently pushed

Blackie down. "I suppose so, James. But it still makes me feel a little sad." She admired the signs James had made and they hurried off to the post office.

"I just hope the manager hasn't changed his mind about helping us," said James as they rang the bell on the door of the small single-story building.

But he hadn't. He even said he'd take a couple of signs to other post offices himself on his way home.

"That's that," said James as they walked back up the path and through the gates. "There's nothing more we can do for now."

"Then let's go to Lilac Cottage," suggested Mandy. "There's an awful lot to tell Grandma and Grandpa about!"

To Mandy's surprise, the sound of country music greeted them as they arrived at the back door of her grandparents' house.

"We're starting square dancing at night at the town hall," explained Grandma after she'd greeted James and Mandy and petted Blackie. "They hold square dances in Walton already and a few members of the badminton club have been going. It seemed silly to have to go there when we can hold our own sessions here."

"That was your grandma's decision, of course," Grandpa smiled. "She's organizing it all."

"Which is why I bought the *Teach Yourself Square Dancing* video," said Grandma, waving toward the television. "I thought I'd better get a little practice in before the first session. But that's enough of my news. Sit down and tell us what's been happening at Animal Ark!"

Twenty minutes later, Grandma's phone rang. "It'll be for you, Dorothy," said Grandpa. "It almost always is."

But when she'd gone to answer the phone, Grandma called from the hall. "It's for you, Mandy. It's Jean Knox. Sounds urgent!"

Mandy leaped to her feet and dashed out, followed closely by James and Grandpa.

"Jean! Jean! How did you know we'd be here? What's wrong? Is Kimble okay? Has something happened to the pups?" Mandy asked the second she had the receiver in her hand.

Grandma, Grandpa, and James waited anxiously to hear what Jean had called about.

"Someone called Animal Ark," Mandy reported quickly, once she'd gotten off the phone. "She said the dog is called Kimble and she likes a warm drink of something called 'Malto' at eight o'clock every night."

"Was that it?" said James. "Nothing else?"

"That was it," replied Mandy. "Jean said she didn't

have time to mention the puppies. She's sure the call came from a phone booth, just like the first one did. That might be to stop us from trying to trace the call."

"It doesn't help, does it?" James sighed as they went back into the kitchen.

"Well, it proves that it was Kimble's owner who left her at the door," said Grandpa. "Nobody else would know to call Animal Ark."

"And we know what to give Kimble to drink," said Mandy. "At least, I think we do. I've never heard of Malto."

"It's a malted powder," said Grandma. "You pour hot milk onto it, like making cocoa, but it's better for dogs. I used to give it to your dad when he was little, Mandy. He loved it. But I haven't seen it for years. I didn't know they still made it."

"We could see if Mrs. McFarlane has any," suggested James.

They said a quick good-bye to her grandparents, James put Blackie on his leash, and they hurried off. "I'll come with you, then take Blackie home," said James.

Mrs. McFarlane ran the Welford general store. Her store sold all kinds of things — a real general store.

The door squeaked loudly when Mandy dashed into McFarlane's. James was tying Blackie up outside; the door squeaked again as he dashed in after Mandy.

"My, you two seem to be in a hurry," said Mrs. McFarlane.

"Hello, Mrs. McFarlane," panted Mandy. "We *are* in a bit of a rush."

"Well, what can I get you then?" The woman smiled.

"Do you sell something called Malto?" asked Mandy.

"It's a malted powder used to make a drink," James put in.

"I don't stock Malto," Mrs. McFarlane told them. "But this makes a malted-tasting drink." She took a can off the shelf and passed it across the counter.

"We could try it, Mandy," said James. "It might taste the same as Malto."

Mandy nodded and gave Mrs. McFarlane some money. "Let's hope it does taste the same," she said.

"Hang on a minute," Mrs. McFarlane called just as Mandy and James were about to leave. "I've just thought of someplace where you might get Malto. I can't remember the name of the store, but it's an old-fashioned specialty drugstore in York. It's down a cobblestone side street just past Mason's, the big furniture store in the main shopping area."

"That's great! Thank you, Mrs. McFarlane," said Mandy.

James nodded in agreement. "If Kimble won't drink

this," he said, "we could catch a train to York tomorrow!"

A few minutes later, Mandy dashed into the clinic. "I've got a malted drink for Kimble," she told Simon breathlessly. "Do you think it'll be okay to give her some?"

"It's worth a try," said Simon. "Your mom looked in on her before she went out on a call. She said Kimble had drunk some water but hadn't touched the milk and sugar. And she still doesn't like anyone getting near her and the pups, Mandy, so I wouldn't talk to her at all. Don't let Blackie anywhere near her, either!"

"It's okay. He's not here," said Mandy. "James is taking him home. So I'll just make the drink, put it as near to the box as I can, and leave Kimble alone."

Before long, Mandy was pouring warm milk onto a tan-colored powder. It smelled very malty and she glanced at the box to see if there was any reaction from Kimble.

Kimble had her head over the side of the box and Mandy was sure the golden retriever's nose was twitching. Moving as casually as she could, Mandy put the bowl on the floor, then went outside.

When James arrived, Mandy was peering in the kitchen window. "I'm watching to see if she'll drink it," she whispered. "She's just getting out of the box, James."

Noses pressed to the window, the two of them watched hopefully as Kimble stretched, then moved toward the bowl. Halfway there, she stopped and turned to look back at the box. Then she moved forward again.

She put her head down to the bowl and sniffed. Her tongue came out and she lapped. But only for a moment. Kimble pushed the bowl away with her nose and walked quickly back to her pups.

Mandy and James sighed so hard that their breath made misty patches on the window.

"So tomorrow morning we go to York!" said Mandy as they turned away. "Because even if anyone calls the SPCA with information about Kimble's owner, Kimble will be with us for a while longer."

"I can't see what good it will do if they do find the owner," said James. "If she'd wanted Kimble back she'd have said so when she called."

But Mandy shook her head. "I *can't* believe she doesn't want Kimble," she said stubbornly. "I'm positive there's a mystery here, James. And somehow we're going to solve it."

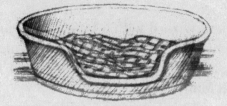

Eleven

"*Apothecary!* Isn't that an old name for a druggist, James?" Mandy pointed to the lettering on the window of a tiny shop on the other side of the narrow cobble-stone street.

"Yes! That's got to be it," said James. He let out a huge sigh of relief. They'd spent over an hour searching the side streets of York for the store. Mrs. McFarlane's instructions on how to find it hadn't been too good.

They crossed the road and pushed open the door, smiling when an old-fashioned bell rang loudly above their heads. The man behind the counter looked like a kindly, ancient wizard with a long gray beard and blue, twinkling eyes. He was very strange looking!

"Hello," said Mandy when she'd found her tongue. "Do you sell Malto?"

"That's an unusual request," said the man. "Normally I'd have to order it specially for you. But you're in luck. I got some in for my one and only regular customer. She's a mail-order customer and I send her half a dozen cans at a time. But she called to say she wouldn't be needing her order just yet. That was Tuesday. So it will be safe to let you have some."

"Could we just have three cans, please?" asked Mandy, her voice high with excitement.

"The box is in the back. I'll go and open it up. Have a look around while you're here. I welcome browsers. People tend to think of me when they want something special or unusual. I stock a lot of old remedies, perfumes, herbs, soap, bath cubes, shaving cream, powdered drinks, licorice roots, herbal candy, cherry gums . . ." He waved in the direction of the tightly packed shelves and went off through a beaded curtain.

Mandy's eyes were shining as she turned to James. "The order was canceled on Tuesday!" she whispered. "*One* day after Kimble was left at the door."

James nodded.

"So are you thinking what I'm thinking?" Mandy asked.

"Yup! His mail-order customer could very well be Kimble's owner. We'll have to turn the conversation to dogs, Mandy, then see what his reaction is. If he's a dog lover he might be willing to tell us something."

When the man appeared with the cans of Malto, Mandy couldn't think of a subtle approach. "Actually, we're buying this for a dog," she told him as she handed him some money. "On Monday night, someone left her at our door with her leash fastened to a heavy flower-pot."

"We thought she might have been stolen, then abandoned," said James. "But nobody's reported her missing. She's a great dog and she's making herself sick pining."

"Then someone called, told us the dog's name, and said she liked Malto. We were wondering" — Mandy gulped before continuing in a rush — "we were wondering if your customer might be the owner!"

The man was silent for a moment. "Hmm. You could be right," he said at last. "She came here once, about a year and a half ago if I remember correctly. I think she did mention that she wanted the Malto for her new puppy. I've been sending it to her ever since."

"That proves it. It is her. It's *got* to be!" Mandy cried, turning to James. "Mom said Kimble is about eighteen months old, didn't she?"

James looked at the man and nodded hard.

"So could you . . . please, could you give us her name and address so we can check?" Mandy asked breathlessly.

The man shook his head. "I'm sorry. I can't possibly give out information like that. It would be a breach of confidence."

"Just the area where she lives would do, sir," said James.

"No. No. I'm sorry. It's out of the question."

"But Kimble might *die* if she keeps pining!" said Mandy. "Could you call her and ask —"

Mandy's plea was interrupted by the ringing of the shop bell. "You'll have to excuse me while I attend to this customer," the shop owner said as an anxious-looking woman hurried in.

"What are we going to do, James?" whispered Mandy. "How can we persuade him to help?"

James gave a deep sigh and shook his head.

As the store owner reached for something from one of the jars behind him, the lady turned to Mandy and James. "I'm sorry if I barged in. My young daughter

doesn't travel very well and I need something for mo-
tion sickness. We've got a long journey ahead of us."

Before Mandy had time to say anything, the door flew
open and a boy about James's age said urgently, "Mom!
Mom! Come quick! Barry's got a bone stuck in his
throat."

"Where is he, Jason? Where have you left him?
Where's Julie?" the woman asked, hurrying toward the
door in a panic.

"I'm here, Mom. What can we do about Barry?" It was
a little girl's voice — high-pitched and frightened.

"We'd better go and see if we can help!" The druggist
came from behind the counter and, followed closely by
James and Mandy, went to the door.

On the sidewalk at the little girl's feet was a small
Yorkshire terrier. Strange bubbling noises came from
his mouth and he was rubbing his face along the
ground.

"Poor Barry!" said the little girl. "He's trying to move
the bone."

"A dog!" said the shop owner, shaking his head. "I
don't think I —"

"A vet! We need a vet!" The lady was crouching down
beside the dog. "I won't be able to remove the bone my-
self!"

Mandy moved swiftly to the distraught woman and crouched down beside her. "Don't worry. I think I can help," she said quietly. She scooped the terrier up into her arms. "Come on, Barry. Let's get you inside."

As Mandy walked to the counter, James cleared a space for the dog. Mandy put the terrier down and James moved to hold his body steady.

"It's all right, boy," Mandy murmured, "I'm going to open your mouth and look at your throat. There's a good dog. It's okay."

"Can you see it? Can you see it? Is Barry going to choke?" the woman asked anxiously.

"It's not a very big bone. Barry picked it up off the street," said Jason.

"Poor Barry!" wailed his little sister. "Can you get the bone out?"

"Shh!" said Mandy. "Please don't talk, you'll make Barry struggle." She looked over to the shop owner. "Could you let me have a pair of tweezers, please?"

"Are you sure you know what you're doing, young lady?"

"Her parents are vets," James told him. "She often helps out in the clinic."

The man pursed his lips, thought for a while, then disappeared through the bead curtain. When he came back he passed Mandy a pair of tweezers.

A couple of minutes later, with a triumphant smile, Mandy placed the small bone on the counter. James stood the terrier up, and the little dog shook his head, then looked at Mandy and yapped.

"Yes! It's gone," she laughed. She turned to the owner and said, "His gums might be a little bit sore but the bone wasn't digging in too much. It was just lodged across his mouth."

Jason moved forward to lift the dog. Then he and his sister cuddled and petted him.

"Thank you so much," their mother said to Mandy and James. "I don't know what we'd have done if you hadn't been here!"

"You're so smart!" said the little girl, looking up at Mandy. "I guess you must like dogs an awful lot."

"I like all animals," Mandy replied with a smile. "And Barry is great," she added, stroking the terrier's head.

"He was naughty, though, picking up that bone," said Julie. "We never let him have little bones like that! We'd better carry him back to the car in case he finds any more."

"Yes, and we'd better hurry," said her mother. "The parking meter will run out."

She paid for her purchase, and after thanking Mandy and James again, the family hurried away.

The store owner looked thoughtfully at Mandy and James. "That was extremely impressive," he said. "You've certainly got a way with dogs, young lady."

"I can't do any more to help poor Kimble, though," said Mandy. "Not unless we can trace her owner and find out why she had to abandon her dog," she added, gazing at him with a look of appeal.

"Hmm. Well. Before you leave, perhaps you wouldn't mind returning the items on my counter to their correct positions!" The man's voice was gruff but his eyes were twinkling. Then he spoke very quickly: "I believe

Kimbleton is a nice town. You should go there some-time."

"Kimbleton?" said Mandy, an idea beginning to dawn.

"That's right," said the man, giving a secret smile.

"I thought Mandy was going to kiss him!" said James. "I had to grab her and get her out of the store."

It was six o'clock. Mandy, her parents, and James were sitting at the kitchen table, watching Kimble drink her second bowl of Malto.

Mandy laughed as she looked at the dog, then toward the door, then back at the dog again. "I thought I was hearing things when the man mentioned a place called Kimbleton. Then to find it's only twenty miles away from us, and that Simon has an aunt who lives there. Oh, I do wish he'd hurry up!" Mandy's eyes swiveled to the door again, willing the nurse to return from calling his aunt.

Dr. Adam smiled and touched his daughter's arm. When she looked at him he put his finger to his lips, then pointed. Kimble was walking slowly toward her.

Mandy hardly dared to breathe; a little earlier when she and James had walked into the kitchen, Kimble had growled at them from the box. But now, was Kimble ready to be friends again?

"Oh, Kimble," Mandy murmured softly as the golden

retriever came and laid her big head on her knee. "It's all right, girl, everything's going to be all right. Will you let me pet you now?"

Mandy slid her hand slowly toward Kimble's nose. Kimble nuzzled into it and wagged her tail. Then she turned and went over to the box. She climbed in, settled down, and licked her two puppies all over.

"Aunt Hannah does know Kimble's owner!" said Simon, coming into the kitchen. "She's named Vera Morley, and she lives alone in an isolated house. Aunt Hannah hasn't seen her for a week or so, but she knew Kimble was having pups so she thought Vera was staying in to be on hand.

"My aunt just can't believe what's happened," Simon continued. "She said Vera thinks the world of Kimble. Apparently, she is a real animal lover, which is how she knew about Animal Ark. Aunt Hannah told her I work here."

"So what do we do now?" asked James.

"We should let the SPCA know and leave it to them," Dr. Adam replied. He glanced at his wife and raised his eyebrows.

"We should," Dr. Emily confirmed. "But maybe this Vera Morley would find it easier to explain things to one of us first."

"Mom!" Mandy leaped up and threw her arms around Dr. Emily's neck.

"It will have to be tomorrow. I'm on call this evening and your dad's got an important meeting."

"And if I don't go now, I'll be late," said Dr. Adam, standing up.

"I promised Aunt Hannah I'd drive over soon for a visit," said Simon. He glanced at Dr. Adam, who smiled. "So it may as well be now," concluded Simon. "Why don't you and James come with me?"

"Simon! You're the best!" cried Mandy. She raced over and gave him a hug.

"Is it okay if I call home, Dr. Emily?" James asked. But his eyes were on Mandy as he moved quickly toward the phone.

Mandy laughed again. "It's okay, James; I won't hug you," she promised.

"From what Simon's aunt said about Vera Morley, it sounds as if something drastic happened to make her leave Kimble here," Dr. Emily warned, her voice serious. "But even if the situation has changed since she left her, the outcome of it all won't be up to us, Mandy. You've got to remember that."

Dr. Emily looked apologetically at Simon. "It's not that I don't trust you, Simon. It's just that I know

Mandy." She turned back to Mandy and said, "So no promising her she can have Kimble back. Is that understood?"

"Yes, Mom," Mandy answered seriously. "I'll be sensible, I promise."

An hour later, Simon pulled his van up outside Vera Morley's house. There were no streetlights in the road, but an old-fashioned lantern hanging outside the porch cast a friendly glow over the large front yard. The house was low and long with two stories and there were lights behind the curtains at the tiny downstairs windows.

"Let me do the talking first, Mandy. Okay?" said Simon as they got out of the van. Mandy nodded and they opened the wooden gate and walked up the path.

Simon knocked on the door, and before long they heard a chain being put into place. The door opened slightly, and a small woman with an anxious look on her face and dark shadows under her brown eyes gazed up at them.

Simon explained quickly that he was Hannah Mitchell's nephew. Vera Morley gasped and her hand went to her mouth.

"The one who works at Animal Ark?" she asked, fumbling to release the door chain. Simon nodded and then introduced Mandy and James.

"You've come about Kimble," said Vera Morley, reaching out for Mandy's hand and almost pulling her in. "Is she all right? Please tell me she's all right. Has she had her puppies? Oh, you've no idea how worried I've been. I couldn't think of any other safe place to take her. I thought . . . I thought it would just be for a day or two . . . but . . . Oh, you must think I'm so irresponsible and uncaring."

"Perhaps we could all go and sit down somewhere where you can tell us about it," suggested Simon.

Vera nodded and led them into the front room.

"I will tell you about it," she said, once they were all sitting around the fire. "But, please, tell me about Kimble first." She pointed to a dog bed on the floor in an alcove next to the hearth. "You've no idea what it's felt like, just staring at Kimble's empty bed night after night, wondering if she was missing me, wondering if she'd had her pups. She's such a softie at times. I knew she'd need me. I promised her I'd be with her when she had her pups."

"We were with Kimble when she had her pups!" James burst out. "Mandy and her mom and me. Kimble was worried and bewildered. Mandy and I held her paw to comfort her, and when she had the puppies she didn't know what to do. We had to show her and help her and —" James broke off suddenly as he noticed the tears rolling down Vera's cheeks.

And when Vera looked across at Kimble's bed and murmured, "Oh, Kimble. I'm so sorry," Mandy's heart went out to her.

"Kimble had four puppies," she said. "There's Jake and Pippa — they're coming along nicely. The third one was stillborn and the fourth one was tiny and weak. We called him Felix. I'm afraid he didn't make it, either."

"But is Kimble all right?" Vera asked, and Mandy glanced across at Simon.

"We think she's going to be now," said Simon. "Dr. Adam and Dr. Emily were worried she'd become dehydrated; she hasn't been eating or drinking as much as she should. But Mandy and James got her some Malto this afternoon, like you suggested, and she had two bowls before we came here."

"Is she enjoying being a mother or is she still feeling too confused?" asked Vera.

"She didn't take to the pups very well at first," said Mandy. "But then . . ." Mandy went on to tell Vera about what happened when Maisy had licked the puppies. "And after that, Kimble became a really loving mom. She was really upset when little Felix died. She wouldn't let anyone go near her or the pups after that."

"Until this evening," said James. "After she'd had some Malto, she went over and put her head on Mandy's knee."

Vera wiped her eyes, then said, "I'll tell you why I left

Kimble. Maybe you'll understand even if you can't for-give me."

Then Vera explained everything.

She told them she rented her house. There was a clause written into the lease stating that no dogs were allowed. But the owner of the house had agreed to waive that clause for Vera.

"Mr. Samuels had known me for a long time," she said. "He knew I wouldn't let a dog wreck the place or go chasing sheep — the fields behind the house belong to a sheep farmer. He got to know Kimble well and he knew my sister, too. She died a year ago. She was blind and her guide dog, a golden retriever related to my Kimble, meant everything to her. She left me some money when she died, and I donated it to the Guide Dog Association. Then I thought it would be nice to let them have a puppy or two to train."

"Did that make you think about letting Kimble have puppies?" Mandy asked. "We guessed the puppies had been planned for."

Vera Morley nodded, then took a quivering breath before continuing. "Mr. Samuels gave me the go-ahead and even said he'd like to adopt one of the puppies. But then . . ."

The rest of the story came out in an anguished rush. A month ago, the landlord had fallen ill and been rushed to the hospital. His nephew had taken over managing the business; Mr. Samuels owned quite a few properties that he rented out. There'd never been anything put in writing about Vera being allowed to keep a dog. The nephew told her she'd have to get rid of Kimble or get out of the house.

"I told the nephew that his uncle had given me permission to have Kimble," said Vera. "But he told me he was in charge now and *he* wasn't giving permission. I ignored him at first. I thought Mr. Samuels would soon be back and it would all blow over. But then the nephew told me his uncle had to have an operation.

"And last Sunday morning he came again and said if Kimble wasn't out of here by the next day, he'd deal with it himself. He said the authorities would be on his side. He said they'd come and take Kimble away!"

"But why didn't you go and see Mr. Samuels?" asked James. "You could have gone on Sunday and he could have explained everything to his nephew!"

"I tried that, James," Vera said, her voice anguished. "Mr. Samuels was very sick. They wouldn't let me see him. I couldn't think of what to do. I knew the nephew would be around first thing the following morning. I was terrified he'd bring someone with him to take Kimble away!"

James took his glasses off and rubbed them furiously

on his sweater while he stared into the fire glowing co-
zily in the hearth.

Vera sighed and ran her fingers through her hair. "In
the middle of the night I suddenly remembered everything Hannah had told me about Animal Ark. I got up
early, put Kimble in the car, and drove toward Welford.
Then, when it was dark, I came and left Kimble at the
door," she whispered. "I thought she'd be safe there for
a day or two while I found somewhere else to live.
When I'd done that I was going to come to Animal Ark
and explain everything."

Vera sighed. "I've spent the whole week going to real
estate agents and calling numbers from newspapers,"
she said. "It was useless. I couldn't find anywhere that
would allow dogs."

"But why didn't you go to Animal Ark and tell
Mandy's parents what was happening?" asked James.
"They might have been able to think of something!"

"Believe it or not, I was going to come this afternoon," said Vera. "I was just about to go out when the
mailman came. He said something about a notice that
had been put up in the local post office late yesterday
afternoon. Said there was a photo of a dog just like Kimble on it, and if anyone knew the dog's owner they were
to inform the SPCA. I don't think he dreamed for a
minute that it *was* Kimble."

She glanced sadly at Simon. "I gave up all hope of everything then. Even if I could find somewhere else to live now, somewhere where I could have Kimble, the SPCA wouldn't let me have her back. Not after I'd abandoned her."

Vera stumbled out of her chair. "I don't know how you found out about me. But I'm grateful to you for coming and for everything you've done for Kimble and her pups. But I'd like you to go now. Give Kimble my love, tell her I miss her, and most of all, tell her I'm sorry I let her down. And please, please, try to find her a good home. And the puppies as well, of course."

Mandy and James looked at Simon for guidance.

Vera looked at Simon, too. "I really do mean it, Simon. There's no other way!"

Twelve

"Do you think we should have left her?" asked Mandy as they walked back down the path. "She was so upset!"

"I know," said Simon. "But I think if we'd stayed she'd have gotten even more upset."

"I think there might be something we can do, though," said Mandy.

James nodded. "I think so, too."

"I'm sure we've all had the same idea," said Simon as he unlocked the van door. "And that's to find out which hospital Mr. Samuels is in!"

"We need to try to get in to see him before we go back

to school on Monday," said James. "We won't have much spare time to do anything."

"We should have asked Vera," said Mandy.

Simon shook his head. "No, we shouldn't have, Mandy. I don't want her to know what we're thinking of doing," he went on. "Because it wouldn't be good to raise her hopes in any way."

"But how are we going to find out where Mr. Samuels is?" asked Mandy.

"I suppose we could call the local hospitals and ask if he's there," said James. "There won't be many, will there?"

"We need a bit more information before we start calling around," said Simon, turning on the ignition. "Knowing Mr. Samuels's first name would help. And my Aunt Hannah is sure to know it! So if you buckle up," he said, pointing to their seat belts, "we'll go and ask her."

"It's almost nine o'clock. Isn't it a little late to go visiting?" asked James.

"Aunt Hannah will be delighted to see us," said Simon.

Simon's Aunt Hannah *was* delighted to see them. She led them into the kitchen and said they were just in time for dinner. She bustled around making hot chocolate, asked Mandy to make herself useful by cutting some fruit, and set Simon and James to work making and buttering toast.

"Eat first, talk after," she commanded when she'd seated them all to her satisfaction. Mandy and James grinned and obeyed willingly when Aunt Hannah added, "Well, get started then. What are you waiting for?"

When they'd finished, Mandy said it was the most delicious supper she could ever remember eating.

James agreed. He'd managed to drink two huge mugs of hot chocolate.

"Good. I'm delighted you enjoyed it! Now, get on with it, Simon," Aunt Hannah said brusquely. "Tell me what happened to make Vera Morley give up the dog she loves."

"I know Kenneth Samuels's nephew," she snorted when Simon had told her everything. "He's a really nasty person. He wants Vera's house for himself. He always has, ever since Vera moved in five years ago."

"I suppose it's too much to hope that you know which hospital Mr. Samuels is in?" Simon asked.

"I saw him this afternoon with my own eyes," his aunt retorted. "I'm a volunteer at Highlands Hospital. Today was my day for visiting. Kenneth is still sick, but not so sick that I couldn't talk with him. There's nobody else to visit him. The nephew doesn't bother and he's Kenneth's only relative."

"Well . . ." Simon began. Then he shook his head. "No," he murmured. "Even you couldn't arrange that!"

"Sure I could. I'm already one step ahead of you."

She looked over at James and Mandy. "Okay, you two. Get some paperback books. And a few flowers, maybe, and some fruit. Be here at two-thirty tomorrow. You two are going to be temporary hospital volunteers. You'll visit folks who don't have anyone else to go to see them."

"Like Mr. Samuels?" asked Mandy.

"That's right!" said Aunt Hannah with a chuckle.

The next day, Mandy and James felt nervous as they followed a nurse down the hospital ward. They were carrying flowers from Grandpa Hope's garden, two jars of raspberry jelly from Grandma's cupboard, and some paperback books that James's father had let them have.

Simon had driven them to his aunt's house and she'd told them that she'd cleared their visit with the head nurse. Mr. Samuels would be expecting them.

But, thought Mandy as they made their way to Mr. Samuels's bed, *he has no idea why we're really here!*

"Think of Vera Morley and Kimble," James whispered. He'd guessed what was worrying Mandy. Mandy nodded and shot him a grateful glance.

"Your young visitors are here, Mr. Samuels," the

nurse said cheerfully. Then she turned to James and Mandy. "Ten minutes. No longer. Okay?"

"Okay," agreed Mandy, hoping that ten minutes would be long enough. There wouldn't be any time to waste!

Mr. Samuels thanked them for their gifts, then looked puzzled. "It isn't often that people your age can find the time to do this kind of thing," he said.

Mandy bit her lip as she met his gaze. "I'm sorry," she said at last. "We *are* here under false pretenses, Mr. Samuels."

"But it's because we're trying to help someone!" James blurted out. Then, blushing boldly, he reached into his pocket, pulled out a photograph, and handed it silently to Mr. Samuels.

"This is Kimble, isn't it? Vera Morley's dog? I'm very, very fond of both of them. I did wonder . . ." Mr. Samuels shook his head. "No reason why she should have come, of course."

"If you're wondering about Vera," Mandy said softly, "she did try to see you, but they wouldn't let her in. You weren't well enough for visitors on the day she came."

"That's a shame. I would have enjoyed a visit from her. She could have told me all about Kimble. Has she had the pups yet? And —"

Mr. Samuels broke off again and looked at James.

"You said you were trying to help someone, young man? I think you'd better tell me what this visit is really about."

"It's about your nephew," James said, getting to the point. "He told Vera Morley that she'd have to get rid of Kimble if she wanted to stay in her house."

"That's ridiculous!" said Mr. Samuels. "Surely she told him that I'd agreed to let her have Kimble there."

"She did!" said Mandy. "And he told her *he* was in charge and he wasn't giving her permission to keep Kimble. He said he'd get the authorities to take Kimble away."

"They haven't done that, have they?" said Mr. Samuels, his face turning red as he sat bolt upright in the bed.

"Not yet," said James. "But they might!" And he and Mandy went on to tell Mr. Samuels everything else that had happened.

"We saw Vera last night and she's given up all hope of having Kimble back," Mandy ended.

Mr. Samuels heaved himself to the edge of his bed and called loudly for a nurse.

"Mr. Samuels! What on earth's the matter?" the nurse asked. "I hope you two haven't been upsetting him," she added, glaring first at James, then at Mandy.

"*You'll* upset me, nurse, if you don't get me to a

phone! I've an important call to make. And you'll have to allow my friends here a few minutes extra with me. We've a very important matter to sort out."

"Are you . . . are you calling your nephew?" Mandy asked when the nurse bustled away to get a wheelchair.

"I'm calling my lawyer. As well as handling my business affairs, he happens to be an old and valued friend. Don't worry, this whole matter will be dealt with immediately!"

Ten minutes later, Mandy and James were dashing across the hospital parking lot to where Simon was waiting by his van.

"So it was a successful visit!" Simon guessed when Mandy and James skidded to a halt.

"Yes! Yes, it was! Mr. Samuels called his lawyer and he's changing Vera's lease," Mandy panted. "She can keep a dog there now."

"And Mr. Samuels's nephew will be getting a letter ordering him to stay away from Vera and her house," added James, shoving his glasses back into place.

"And . . . and first thing tomorrow Mr. Samuels and his lawyer will be calling the SPCA inspector who handles cases in the Kimbleton area," said Mandy. "They'll both explain what happened and Mr. Samuels will —"

"Vouch for Vera. That's the word he used," said James.

"The SPCA *will* agree to let Vera have Kimble back, won't they, Simon?" Mandy asked anxiously.

"I think so," Simon replied thoughtfully. "But they're bound to pay her a visit to check everything out."

The next three days passed slowly. Vera called every day to check on Kimble and the pups; she was becoming more and more anxious because she hadn't heard anything from the SPCA.

Then, on Thursday, when Mandy and James came home from school, Dr. Emily was parked outside in the Animal Ark Land Rover. "Throw your bikes in the back," she said. "We're going to Kimbleton. I've checked with your mother, James, and it's all right for you to come."

"But *why*?" asked Mandy. "Why are we going, Mom? What's happened?"

"Vera Morley's had a visit from the SPCA inspector," Dr. Emily told them. "She called Animal Ark to ask if you two could go to lend support. Now, Mandy, you've got to promise me that you'll accept whatever is said. No protest if the decision goes against Vera. Okay?"

"But, Mom . . ." began Mandy. Then she relented. She knew from the seriousness of her mother's expression that she meant exactly what she'd said. "Okay," she whispered. "I promise."

"Me, too," murmured James. "But it *will* be all right, won't it, Dr. Emily?"

"I don't know the answer to that, I'm afraid, James. We'll just have to hope it will be."

There was already a car there when they drove up to Vera's house. Mandy didn't know whether to be glad or not.

"If that's the inspector's car, at least we won't have to wait long before we know!" muttered James.

When Vera opened the front door, Mandy looked anxiously at her, trying to judge how things were going. Vera looked pale and worried and didn't speak. She just pointed silently toward the front room.

Dr. Emily introduced herself, Mandy, and James to the stern-faced inspector.

"I was about to impress upon Ms. Morley the possible consequences of abandoning an animal," he said. "It doesn't matter that she did her best to make sure the dog was unable to run off. It could have run off when the leash was unfastened. That could have caused an accident, even death, not only to the dog but to whoever was trying to help the dog. In other words, leaving a dog, even at the door of a veterinary practice, was a highly irresponsible act."

"I know that," Vera whispered. "I know I should have

taken Kimble and asked for help. But what if the answer had been no? What would I have done then?"

The clock ticked away as the inspector and Vera sat in silence. Then came a loud cock-a-doodle-doo and Vera rose to her feet. "I'm sorry," she said. "The hens need feeding and to be put in for the night. It's well past time."

"Tell us where everything is and James and I will take care of it," said Mandy. She didn't really know how she could bear to leave the room without any decision having been made. But the hens were hungry and their routine had been upset.

Before Vera could reply, the inspector turned to look at Dr. Emily. "Are the dog and her pups well enough to be moved?" the inspector asked Dr. Emily.

Moved to where? Mandy wanted to ask the question aloud but she knew she couldn't. She only vaguely heard her mother's confirmation; she was watching Vera stumbling back to her chair.

"Perhaps, Mandy, when you and James have fed the hens, you'd like to go back to Animal Ark in Ms. Morley's car," said the inspector. "I'm sure she'd like to get Kimble and the puppies and get them settled in their own home as soon as possible."

To Mandy's horror, Vera Morley said, "No, Inspector. I won't be going to Animal Ark. Not today," she added quickly, wiping away the tears. "Tomorrow morning, can I come tomorrow morning?" she asked Dr. Emily. "The waiting will be awful but I wouldn't dare bring them home in the dark. I'd be scared of having an accident."

"Come back with us now, Vera," said Dr. Emily. "You can stay the night. I'm sure Mandy will be delighted," she added, throwing a smiling glance at her daughter. "You can sleep in the spare room."

As they walked down the hallway to Animal Ark's kitchen, they heard anxious and excited whines and frantic scratching noises at the closed door.

"She's recognized my footsteps!" cried Vera, running forward. "I'm coming, Kimble. I'm here!"

The whines turned to yelps of joy when Vera opened the door. Kimble didn't jump up; she didn't need to. Vera knelt down and flung her arms around Kimble's neck. In between whining and yelping, Kimble licked Vera's face and neck and ears.

Mandy, James, and Dr. Emily stood in the hall, smiling as they watched the reunion.

"Oh, Kimble! Kimble," Vera murmured. The dog stayed still for a moment, her big golden head resting on Vera's shoulder.

Then Mandy drew a sobbing breath and whispered,

"Mom! Kimble's crying. I didn't know a dog could cry real tears."

"Oh, dear," said Emily Hope. "I think I need a tissue."

"Me, too," said James, taking off his glasses and blinking hard.

Then Kimble moved. She got hold of Vera's jacket in her mouth and started tugging. "I think she wants to show Vera her puppies," said James. "I don't want to miss this. Will it be okay if we go in, Dr. Emily?" Dr. Emily nodded.

Kimble's tail was wagging furiously as she led Vera to the box. Vera knelt down again, and after murmuring something to Kimble, she picked the puppies up. "They're beautiful, Kimble," she said as she petted and examined them.

Kimble lay down and put her head on Vera's knee. "What did you say you call the puppies, Mandy?" Vera asked over her shoulder. "Jake and Pippa?"

"Yes, but we won't mind if you want to rename them," Mandy replied.

"Oh, no!" said Vera. "We couldn't do that, could we, Kimble? Just move your head for a second, girl. I'll put your pups back, then I want another look at you. I've missed you so much."

Vera leaned forward and lay the puppies down.

"There you are, Jake," she said. "You snuggle close to Pippa."

As Vera waited to make sure the puppies were settling in, James glanced at Kimble. The dog's eyes were fixed adoringly on Vera.

James took a huge, long breath, then turned to Mandy and said, "I'm going now, Mandy. I think I want to get home and spend some time with Blackie." He gave a last, lingering look at Kimble, saying a silent but happy good-bye.

Vera didn't sleep in the spare room after all but on a cot in front of the stove in Animal Ark's kitchen. She just couldn't bear to be parted from Kimble. Kimble and the puppies slept on the cot, too. Vera apologized about that when Mandy crept into the kitchen early Friday morning.

"I tried to make Kimble keep Jake and Pippa in the box," she said. "But every time I moved them, she just picked them up and put them on the cot again."

"It's okay," said Mandy, smiling as she looked down at the contented family. Then she looked closer. "Vera," she whispered, "the puppies' eyes are starting to open! I'm sure they are. It must be because they know they're going home."

*   *   *

Three weeks later, Mandy heard a muffled thump coming from outside the front of the house. She opened the door to find Kimble standing here. But this time, the dog at the door wasn't tied to a flowerpot. She was holding a small card in her mouth.

Mandy bent down to cuddle Kimble, then, keeping one arm around the dog's neck, she removed the card and read it. *"Vera Morley and Kenneth Samuels request the pleasure of Mandy Hope's and James Hunter's company at their wedding . . ."*

Mandy stood up with a smile of delight as Vera and Mr. Samuels, each carrying a wriggling puppy, came from behind a bush. "You will accept, won't you, Mandy?" asked Vera, blushing a becoming shade of pink. "You and James *will* come to our wedding?"

"Of course we will!" said Mandy, moving forward to pet the puppies.

"And," Mandy said to James when she called him later, "I know just where we can go to buy Vera and Mr. Samuels a wedding present. A little old-fashioned apothecary in York!"

Look for Animal Ark®:
HORSE IN THE HOUSE

Each time the auctioneer glanced at his list, Mandy expected to hear Matty's name over the loudspeaker.

"It's exciting, isn't it?" said James. "I mean, even though we feel sorry about Wilfred and everything."

Mandy nodded in agreement. "There are more horses here than at the Welford Show."

All kinds of horses could be seen, from mild-natured, sturdy Welsh ponies to sleek, hot-blooded Thoroughbreds. *But none of them is as lovely as gentle, silver-coated Matty*, thought Mandy.

Two hours passed before Mandy glanced up at a wall clock. She was beginning to get hungry. She resisted the temptation to eat the apple that she had snatched quickly on the way out of Animal Ark and stuffed in her pocket. It was a good-bye treat for Matty.

"And now the first of a number of horses from the highly reputable Bennetts' Riding Stables."

"Here they come at last," said James. He didn't look excited now, just subdued and a little sad.

Mandy felt the same. She set her shoulders and looked over the barrier.

"We'll begin with Star — a ten-year-old mare."

As Star was led into the ring, Mandy saw the ripple of interest run through the buyers. "Who'll start the bidding?" the auctioneer asked again. Mandy tensed. This was it. It might be the last time she saw any of the Bennetts' horses, including Matty. She found herself longing to see her. The bidding for Star was fierce, with voices seeming to come from everywhere. Suddenly the hammer hit the gavel. "To you, sir!" And Star was sold.

"And now we have Socks. Also from the Bennetts' stable. Who'll start me at . . ."

Socks — with the two white feet — pranced around the ring, looking unconcerned about all the commotion. He, too, was sold quickly. Then came graceful Bella. The bids came fast, while the auctioneer noted each one, tapping at the air with his pen.

"Any more bids? Do we have the last bid? Sold to you, sir!"

"Goodness!" said James. "They don't waste any time, do they?"

"No," Mandy replied. "That's because Wilfred's horses are so good."

It was true. Muscles moved fluidly beneath the glossy coats, heads were held high, and ears pricked intelligently. Despite her feelings about the sale, Mandy felt proud for Wilfred. His horses were so beautiful. "A credit to him," her grandma would have said.

Mandy wished each horse luck. "Good-bye. I hope you'll be happy in your new home," she whispered.

Next to be announced was Wilfred's sturdy brown pony, Treacle. Treacle trotted around the ring, his tail swishing back and forth. Like the horses before him, he was bursting with good health.

"No Matty yet," James said, echoing Mandy's thoughts.

"No," she replied, half-dreading, half-longing to catch a glimpse of the gray mare. How many horses was that so far — four? Four more to go.

James tapped her on the arm. "See that man over there? He's bought all of Wilfred's horses up to now."

Mandy looked across at the man. She read the large

card he held up to the auctioneer as he bought Treacle. "Newcombe," she read aloud. It wasn't a local name.

"Who is that, Dad?" she asked, when Dr. Adam paused for a minute near the barrier during a break in the bidding.

"Jim Newcombe," Dr. Adam answered. "He owns large riding stables near York. He's well-respected and takes excellent care of his horses."

"Oh." Mandy was relieved. At least Wilfred's horses would be well treated.

As the auction resumed, Dr. Adam went back over to the pens.

"And now, the fifth horse on sale today from Bennetts' stables," said the auctioneer over the loudspeaker. "Where will we start the bidding for Blaze — a handsome fifteen-year-old?"

Mandy tightened her fingers on the barrier. Just three more of Wilfred's horses to be sold: William, Honey, and Matty. Who would be next? Honey's name rang out and the sandy-colored mare lifted her head and whinnied as she was led around the ring. Then came the sound of the hammer hitting wood again. That was it.

"Two left now," Mandy breathed. Suddenly, her throat felt tight with unshed tears. It was almost over. She wondered what Wilfred was thinking.

"That Newcombe man bought Blaze and Honey as well," James said. "He must have tons of money."

"I hope he's got enough left to buy William and Matty, too," Mandy responded, crossing her fingers for luck. *I'll give Matty a final hug when I give her the apple*, she thought.

The loudspeaker crackled to life again. "And now the seventh and last of the horses from Bennetts' Stables. William is a nine-year-old gelding. . . ."

Mandy's eyes widened in surprise. That couldn't be right. William wasn't the *last* of Wilfred's horses. There was still Matty to come.

"Hey! What's going on?" said James.

"I don't know," Mandy replied.

They waited expectantly while William was led around the sale ring. The auctioneer acknowledged the last few bids. "Any more? Do we have the last bid? Sold to Mr. Newcombe! That was the final horse from Bennetts' Stables. And now we have Bruce. A Shetland pony . . ."

Mandy looked at James. "But what about *Matty*?"

He shook his head, as surprised as she was.

Mandy was too stunned to react at first. Then worry began creeping in. Where could Matty be? Suddenly she knew what she must do: "I've got to find Wilfred," she said.

"But your dad told us to stay right here," James reminded her.

Mandy hesitated. Her dad's instructions had been clear and she didn't want to get into trouble, but she just had to find out what had happened to Matty.

"Look, Wilfred's just over there," she said, catching sight of the stooping figure. "I won't be long. I'll be back before Dad comes over here to get us."

Some of the buyers moved back to let her pass, but others glared down at her disapprovingly. Mandy bent and made herself as small as she could and squeezed her way through the crush of people.

It was a few minutes before she managed to get through the crowd. "Wilfred! Mr. Bennett!" she called in an urgent whisper.